WHAT HAPPENED TO SERENITY?

PJ Sarah Collins

Red Deer PRESS

*Much of the greatness of the human spirit
can be seen in our passionate pursuit
of knowledge, truth, justice, beauty, perfection, and love.
At the same time, few things are so haunting
as the stories of the very greatest seekers falling short.*

Os Guiness, from *The Call*

Published by Red Deer Press
A Fitzhenry & Whiteside Company
195 Allstate Parkway, Markham, ON, L3R 4T8
www.reddeerpress.com

Edited for the Press by Peter Carver
Cover and text design by BookWorks
Cover Image Courtesy iStock
Printed and bound in Canada by Webcom

5 4 3 2 1

We acknowledge with thanks the Canada Council for the Arts, and the Ontario Arts Council for their support of our publishing program. We acknowledge the financial support of the Government of Canada through the Book Publishing Industry Development Program (BPIDP) for our publishing activities.

ONTARIO ARTS COUNCIL
CONSEIL DES ARTS DE L'ONTARIO

Canada Council
for the Arts

Conseil des Arts
du Canada

Library and Archives Canada Cataloguing in Publication

Collins, P. J. Sarah, 1971-
What happened to serenity / P.J. Sarah Collins.
ISBN 978-0-88995-453-3
I. Title.

PS8605.O47W43 2011   jC813'.6   C2011-901434-3

Publisher Cataloging-in-Publication Data (U.S)

Collins, PJ Sarah.

What happened to Serenity / PJ Sarah Collins.

[ ] p. : cm.

Summary: Katherine lives in complete isolation in a post-apocalyptic community. Knowledge and the search for truth are not permitted. A haunting story about growing up and searching for truth.

ISBN: 978-0-88995-453-3 (pbk.)

1. Science fiction – Juvenile literature. 2. Values – Juvenile fiction. I. Title.
[Fic] dc22   PZ7.C6554Wh 2011

Preserving our environment

Red Deer Press chose to print the pages of this book on recycled paper and saved these resources[1]:

	energy	water	greenhouse gases	solid waste
	10 million BTUs	56,658 L	1,410 kg	412 kg

33 trees were saved for our forests

Printed by **Webcom Inc.** on Legacy Hi-Bulk Natural 100% post-consumer waste.

ANCIENT FOREST™ FRIENDLY

FSC
www.fsc.org
MIX
Paper from responsible sources
FSC® C004071

[1]Estimates were made using the Environmental Defense Paper Calculator.

Acknowledgements

I would like to thank:

Curtis, Isaiah, Elena, and Moses;

Peter Carver, for transforming this story into a book;

Alison Acheson, for insight and support from the very beginning;

Laura Peetoom, for input on an earlier draft;

Workshop suggestions from fellow writers including: Kari-Lynn Winters, Mary Razzell, Kallie George, and Michelle Davis.

Dictionary references in Chapter Seven are from the *Thorndike Barnhart Comprehensive Desk Dictionary*, Doubleday & Company, Inc., Garden City, New York, 1955.

Part of the author's proceeds from sales of this book are being donated to BC Children's Hospital Foundation.

Prologue
Monday, August 9, 2021

Everything is not as it seems.
I've seen the outside come
Through the sky.

I find the words scribbled on a piece of paper, hidden inside a metal box in the cornfield, one of its corners sticking out of the earth. It seems it's only partly buried so that it can be easily found. I'm looking for my best friend, Anna, who I think might be hiding, but I find the box instead. There is something familiar about the handwriting.

I believe what it is saying. It confirms what I've suspected for a long time.

What did the note writer see?

My teachers tell me that polite people do not ask questions, that I should release my individual thoughts and focus on our Manifesto. I wonder what it would be like to use questions as a part of normal speech. I wish I could talk openly with my parents about the note, but we don't ever do that as a family. My parents only care about one thing since I started my last level in school.

Their voices echo in my head.

"Don't ask questions and you'll get assigned a good Role after Harvest Break," Mom says.

"Listen to your mom," Dad grumbles. "It's for the best."

"Release for peace," Sister Margaret chimes.

As I bury the box in the cornfield, I realize that sometimes it hurts to be right.

I'm fifteen and alone with a terrible secret.

1

Tuesday, August 10, 2021

My mind is racing when I wake up the next morning. I lie in bed, in the darkness, as sparrows chirp somewhere in the roof, and think about the note inside the metal box. Who wrote the note?

I realize, then, what is familiar about the handwriting: it reminds me of Dad's ... the same small, tight letters. But that can't be. Should I tell Anna what I found?

Anna and I have been best friends since we were in Level One but, lately, I've felt us growing apart. She still thinks that the Community is perfect, just as they tell us. I confide in her about the problems I see, but that only seems to strengthen her faith in the Manifesto.

"It bothers me that Father is the only person allowed to ask questions," I tell her.

"His questions are for our good, for the purpose of medicine," she recites, then says, "Father asks questions as our doctor."

"When I ask questions, I'm rude; and when he does, it's allowed. There's something strange about that."

"It's natural to outgrow questions, Katherine," Anna insists. "Don't fight it."

I'd tell her about the box, but she'd just tell me it was a Senior boy's idea of a joke and that I always jump to crazy conclusions.

I get up and pull back the thick, brown drapes. The hot morning sun streams into my small bedroom, bringing light to every corner. Outside, I see Dad's brown hat bob up and down among the stalks of wheat as a light wind swirls around him. He's always up before the dawn; it's when he feels most alive. But in this, as in most things, I'm his opposite.

I close my window and pull the drapes. My best chance for keeping this room cool for bedtime is to block the sunlight during the day.

I make the bed with the pink and purple quilt that Mom and I stitched together during Snow Break. I study the intricate pattern of triangles while I brush my long, light brown hair. Then I look into the tiny looking glass nailed to the wall and examine my face. My brown eyes look smaller this morning, my face freckled and tanned. Nothing like Anna's tightly coiled black hair, high forehead, and dark, dimpled complexion. I pinch my cheeks and turn away. Anna is so beautiful.

As carefully as she would, I dress in my beige summer uniform, and then pull out my small, purple writing book from under my mattress. My hands are always slow to open the thick and bumpy paper cover, stained with blackberry juice. Two winters ago, Mom and I sieved the paper pulp, but found it took days to dry. Impatient, we dehydrated the paper—actually, flipped it like flapjacks—on top of the crackling cast-iron stove.

My parents' beliefs are very confusing. They break rules and create secret color. They are sparing with their rations so they can make things for themselves, things they don't share with the Community, *individual* things.

But if I dare to ask Mom a question, as I did last night during my chores, she sends me to bed without dinner, without my getting a chance to watch the Remote. If the Manifesto was really so important to my parents, I think they would follow all of it.

I flip through the worn pages to a fresh one. On it, I record today's date and what I read on the cornfield note. I can't remember the exact wording, but I think I'm really close. Then I turn back to something I wrote last winter.

October 22, 2020

When first flakes fall
We stop what we are doing
As if already frozen.
And even though we know
That bitter cold is coming
For some reason
We smile
And run outside
Dancing.

I still remember the morning this early snow surprised us. We woke up to Dad's yipping through the house. How happy he was that the harvest had been safely gathered and his repairs to the sod roof were newly complete. He danced Mom around the kitchen, then straight into the snow off the porch. She chided him for soaking her secret, red wool slippers, even though she couldn't hide her laughing eyes from me.

I turn back a few pages to last summer.

July 11, 2020

> *Today the Community women gathered saskatoons for jam. I picked out the stems until both hands were purple and sticky. I threw the green ones at Mom and she giggled like a girl. Under the table, I found Scott, holding his stomach, his clothes covered in stains, an empty, tipped-over bucket nearby.*

Usually I smile when I read this, but today it makes me feel sad. It seems so long since Mom and I enjoyed each other. Lately, she's always picking at me to change. And I don't know how to do that, not in the way that would make us both happy.

I put my book under the mattress in its safe place and hide all my color under the plain brown quilt. I turn back at the door, just to be sure that it's all as it should be.

Mom is in the kitchen, making bread. She looks surprised to see me up so early. Her brow is lightly dusted with coarse rye flour and she is pounding a small doughy batch onto the wood countertop.

I make a comment about how much better her bread is than the loaves we get through rations, which Mom thinks are only passable for stuffing or bread pudding. My mom would rather use up her flour allocations this way, with fresh homemade bread in the mornings, than save it for anything else. My stomach rumbles and I look for something to nibble.

Mom isn't tempted into light conversation. "Good morning, Katherine," she says, pursing her lips.

I know what is expected of me. "I'm sorry I was rude last night."

She stops kneading the dough and rests her petite hands on the counter. "Really, Katherine. Your questions are becoming more frequent instead of disappearing altogether."

"I upset you and Dad. I see that. I am sorry."

"You are only sorry because you upset your parents." Mom often repeats things I say in order to get more information.

But I am silent now.

"Questions are a rude and primary way of seeking information. You know that. You've heard it a thousand times," she pleads.

A hundred thousand. Twenty times a day. I've been counting.

"I can't help it."

"Don't lie." She starts pounding the dough again and her long brown hair sways with the effort. "You show respect for the Brothers and Sisters by accepting what they tell you. You're a young woman now."

"So I'm too old for answers?"

Mom drops the dough ball onto the counter. "Katherine!"

Can I really not help it? What's wrong with me? I lower my head and am quiet. She doesn't understand me.

Mom takes my silence as submission. She washes her hands in the basin and hugs me from behind, her head resting between my shoulder blades.

I used to love Mom's arms around me. And now, for a second, I feel safe. She turns me around and her still wet hand gently reaches to touch my cheek.

"Eugenia, Prudence, and Anna all stopped asking questions months ago. Your teachers are worried about you," she says softly.

Brother Michael? Sister Margaret? Worried? I'm confused. This is the first time in ten years of school that I've heard this. How can this be? I'm always the smartest in my level. I pull back from Mom's touch.

"And in the library, my dearest friend Sister Millie said that even the Junior boys don't ask questions anymore." Mom takes me by the shoulders and grips hard. Her breath reminds me of chamomile. "If you can behave and get a good Role, you can have a better life than mine. After Harvest Break is finished, you could be happy in your Life Role, maybe thinking about marriage. There are some nice Senior boys in your class."

I shake my head.

"You look as if you just smelled curdled milk. Some older boys, then. There were some strong, handsome ones at the Lake Festival. They would make good husbands. I saw you looking."

"They were competing in Log Skills. *Everyone* was looking."

She pauses. I look away and Eric's face flashes briefly into my mind.

"Father wants to see you. This week sometime."

The head of the Community wants to see me? Am I in real trouble, then? Hot blood blushes my face. Does he know that I found the box? Of course not, right? Why do I always jump to crazy conclusions?

Mom walks back to the dough.

I start to panic. "But I'm not sick. Why does he want to see me?"

"Really, Katherine. There you go again."

I can't even ask for help! I bite my lip, drawing a bit of blood, then exhale in frustration and cross my arms. I don't understand her.

"You can forget about any Remote this week. Think about your future instead and how you want to spend your last few weeks in this home before you get your Life Role. Now, go prepare your brother for school and see to your morning chores."

My brother, Scott, is my favorite person on the planet. My parents lost four others in between the two of us, after trying seven years to have a child. Sometimes I think he's *their* favorite, but that usually doesn't bother me. Scott is six years old and sometimes, when our parents watch the Community Report on Remote, we play chess.

On our walks to school, we talk the whole way—that is, if we're not counting the sunflowers that line both sides of the lane, which we often do. He knows that it's not appropriate to ask questions, but he can't help himself, either. He gets away with it because underneath his beige, primary summer hat, he has eyes the color of the sky and hair like wheat.

"You missed a good show: puppets and music." He dances on ahead of me, then stops. "Why couldn't you watch the Kids Hour with me?"

"I talk too much."

Scott smirks. "You missed the red light. Came on halfway through the show."

Ah … the red beam that goes right through your eyes to fill your senses, so peaceful and serene. "I wish I was there, then."

"I love red," Scott says as he picks at some dandelions in the dirt road.

"Me, too." I'm not asking Scott questions today on purpose. I'm trying to be a good example.

"Why is everything beige and browns?"

I quote part of the Manifesto: "Brown is our Community; We versus I. Brown is everything the Community owns together. Brown lets us blend into our natural environment and resembles the dirt we will someday become."

Scott isn't satisfied. "I would rather have red and yellow crayons than beeswax and walnut ones."

He's a creative child. But I would rather read or write than draw pictures. Most of the books in the library are stories about our Community, but there is a small novel and poetry section, all of which I've read. There used to be other books, too, old books like the ancient split dictionary that Sister Millie was going to have pulped before I saved it and tucked it under my mattress. We used to have stories that were written before the Ecological Revolution, but they are long gone, somewhere.

"What is your Role going to be, Katherine?"

"Anything with books, I hope." Might Sister Millie pick me as her apprentice? Would it appear improper or partial to pick her best friend's daughter for such an honor? Is the Community even large enough to spare two workers in this Role? And would Father see a need to expand and refine the Library's collection of books?

Scott touches each sunflower with a stick as he walks.

"Where do the books come from?"

"You know, from trees or crops—wood or plant pulp. A few

people write, illustrate, print, and bind them. It's a lot of work." I remember this from a Level Six project.

"My class is going to the forest soon," Scott tells me. "My teacher, Sister Lucia, says there are big and little trees there."

"Right. They plant the small trees to replace the ones they cut down."

"I know. And she says that lots of things are made from wood: toys, paper, houses, even warm."

I correct him on this. "You mean wood is also a fuel."

"Yes, but you need a fire before you can have the warm."

"Warmth."

"Yup. Is the Remote made from wood?"

I'm interested in what he's thinking. "What do you mean?"

Scott kicks at a stone. "I know the box is wood, and the dark glass is from the Community Glassworks. But when I look in close, I see some colored wires. Who makes those?"

"They are collected from materials in the warehouse. It's someone's Role. In Level Six you'll learn them all and you'll start more projects in the warehouse, like the big boys."

"And it seems like magic to me, that the Remote could work at all. Why does it turn on in the evening without anyone asking it to?"

He notices contradictions, too. I've wondered about the Remote many times.

"Father knows best. He signals it to turn on at the right time so we can be connected with each other—with our entire Community."

I can tell Scott isn't satisfied, but I don't want him talking like this to anyone else. I kneel and take my brother by the hand, tilting the sunhat so I can see his rosy face, his twinkling sky eyes. "Listen, Scott. Let's just make this our secret. Let's only talk like this together."

Scott smiles his widest, gap-toothed grin and nods. He enjoys games.

We enter the schoolyard. He kisses me goodbye, leaving my cheek wet from his sloppy puppy dog lips.

I watch him run towards the Boys' Building.

A stick cracks underfoot; I turn and freeze.

"Hi," Eric says, walking over, hands in pockets. He half-smiles, then looks down, his cheeks flushed, as if he has been running.

I nod and try to say his name but no sound squeaks out.

"Your lace is untied," he tells me, then proceeds to tie it up for me, the curls of his russet-colored hair brushing the hem of my knee-length skirt.

I swallow and stop breathing; my stomach flips.

He stands then, his head just taller than mine. He looks through me with gray-green thoughts I can't map, his eyes framed by thick, dark lashes. He's so close, I can't even look away or my forehead will bump his chin. He has freckles, real faint ones on his nose, and he smells clean and sweet, like new beeswax soap.

He takes a step back, then moves next to me, and I exhale.

"Thanks," I whisper.

We both stand there for a few seconds, as if not sure what to say next.

"No Anna, yet," he says finally, his hands back into his pockets.

I look around, see other girls from my level, but he's right, no Anna. Instead, Eric is here today, for the very first time—just to meet me.

His shoulder nudges mine, and I look at it, and then look away, my cheeks hot.

"We should be at the lake in this heat," he says, and the thought makes my spine tingle. *We.*

I take a deep breath, then say, "I'm surprised to see any Junior or Senior boys here at all. Thought you'd all be at the warehouse, reinventing the old technology or building some—"

Eric's hand brushes mine and I look down. He's standing so close.

"No, I expect we'll be haying most of the week," he says.

I try to think of something interesting to say. "Well, that's summer school—endless jobs to keep us busy until Harvest Break, when the top four levels assist the adults." I'm babbling. Has he noticed?

"Next year—next month—will be different. I can't wait," he says. "You and I will get good Roles; we're both expected to lead our levels."

The bell rings then, and he shocks me—he takes my hand, then kisses me full on the mouth. He lingers a sweet second, then pulls away, walking backwards towards the school, playful eyes still on me, grinning sheepishly.

"Gives me something to think about until then," he says, with a wink. Then he turns and runs off.

Field mouse, you
A brown-grey surprise
Scampering towards me
Staring, watching
Head on an angle.
Blue sky
Sunlight streaming down
Casting morning shadows.
A Blue Jay calls
And you disappear again
As if we never met.

2
Tuesday Morning, August 10, 2021

I watch Eric leap the stairs to the Boys' Buildings, then close my lips.

All the way to Room Three, my mind is amazed and my nerves still tingle. I sit in my seat, dazed, half crazy. Did that really just happen? I'm bursting to tell Anna, though she'd probably just repeat what she said before: "You two have been looking at each other in the blushing way since the start of the year." I can't wait to tell her that shy Eric is full of surprises.

But she's not in school today and she's never late. I try to recall the last time she was away, but can't remember back that far. Brother Michael and Sister Margaret, the teachers for our multi-leveled room for Levels Seven to Ten, seem preoccupied. They whisper and look at Anna's empty chair. They tell the younger kids to braid candlewicks while the Juniors and Seniors complete Dowry Stitching Projects.

I can't concentrate. I decide to go and see Anna during the lunch break. If I run, I can make it to her house in fifteen minutes.

All morning, my mind flips from Eric to Anna to the note. I

have a hard time focusing during our Naturopathy class. My Home Chemistry equations take me twice as long to finish. If my teachers notice, they don't say anything. I'm agitated by the time it's Dictation, but for thirty minutes, I must settle my thoughts to absorb Sister Margaret's lesson on air travel for the afternoon Fact Drill.

She drops her notes, and bends to pick them up, her wide bottom facing us. Someone giggles. She stands quickly then, and looks down to reorganize her papers, but her long black hair slips to block her view. She flicks most of it back over her shoulder, and her moon face and deep eyes rise to face us. She clears her throat and, on cue, we lift our pencils.

"Fact. Before the Ecological Revolution in 1979, people and cargo were mainly transported across the globe by ships, trucks, and planes," she says in her singsong voice.

Sometimes I wish learning in school was more relevant. It's just a matter of time now before Sister Margaret reminds us again that air travel is impossible due to earth's unstable atmosphere. But then, why don't migrating birds and geese have a problem with unstable air? Or do they? What's really true?

"Fact. Aircraft not only used immense amounts of fossil fuels, they also were a drain on the environment in air quality and land use. Air strips were not an ecologically sustainable way of managing land, or of fitting in with surrounding natural ecosystems."

Our Dictation lessons are usually facts about life before the Ecological Revolution. Why do teachers torture us with facts that we can never test for ourselves?

When we're dismissed for lunch, I hurry out the door. I'm hoping to avoid Eugenia and Prudence, who will want to share gossip or watch boys. Anna and I always avoid them by running into the cornfield. Oh, how I love summer. Mature crop fields and lots of places for our imaginations to burn trails.

But something is different when I enter the yard. The older boys surround Brother Joshua and receive instruction about something.

I spot Eric, then slip around the Girls' Building toward the road that leads to Anna's house. As soon as I'm out of view, I start to jog.

Within ten minutes or so, I'm in the area where people live who do not require land to do their Life Roles. Anna's dad helps in the peat bogs after spring thaw, the Cannery through the summer, and manages fuel rations throughout the winter.

The houses here are brown and identical in shape to the farm-houses and have few distinguishing features. Some have little flower patches between them, one with some large red dahlias and sweet pea vines. In front of all the houses is a huge rectangular Community Tea and Herb Garden. I recognize the fragrances of rosehip, peppermint, and parsley, but there are many more plants. The grass in front of each house has been shortened with a rolling grass cutter.

To my left, I see the half-finished Uncles and Aunts Memorial Garden. There was a time when Father could not bear to see this con-structed, and the surprise gift for him, unveiled last Harvest—a large wooden statue of a man and a toddler—caused him great sadness. He wept such tears, so the carving was hastily re-veiled. However, I've since overheard some women say that perhaps this Spring, after plant-ing, it might be completed—with Father's approval first, of course.

I enter the trim yard in front of Anna's house and knock on the front door. No one answers immediately, although I hear shuffling inside and see window curtains move.

Finally, the door opens.

Anna's eyes are red and puffy from crying, her clothing sloppy and disheveled.

"Anna!" What is going on?

"Oh," she says, her shoulders slumping, and she almost tips over towards me.

I reach to steady her, but her body shakes. I hold her tighter and wait until big, silent tears wet my shoulder and she finds her strength again. And as she cries, everything I wanted to tell her about Eric seeps away. It doesn't matter anymore, not compared to this.

"I have to go," she says.

"What …" I say, but then stop. I don't have a right to this information. Maybe I'm intruding and being rude, like Mom tells me. But couldn't asking be a way of caring?

Anna motions her finger to her lips, steps out onto the porch and closes the door.

"It's all over. My life is over."

I stare at her, puzzled.

"My sister, Serenity … has disappeared."

Disappeared? Gone?

"No," I say, shaking my head. "You mean lost." Were the boys being organized into search parties? Is that why they were gathered together in the yard?

"Last night, my parents and I woke to a noise outside. Dad went to check on it while Mom and I looked in on the others. We checked every room, under every piece of furniture, in every possible place, but Serenity …" Anna crumples onto the porch and sobs.

"Tell me," I implore, dropping down next to her.

Anna flops her hands to the porch. "She fell asleep after dinner, then a noise woke us up in the night—and now she's gone. That's all I know."

"Does Serenity sleepwalk? Does she wake at night?"

Anna starts crying louder, ignoring my questions. "We've been looking since two in the morning. We've looked everywhere." The tears run down her nose, wetting her brown apron.

I cry, then, too. How could this happen? Was a wolf near the outhouse?

"I'm sure they'll find her," I tell Anna.

"I can't talk. Father is upstairs, collecting the details from my Mom and Dad. I should make him tea or something." She stands up. "My parents are so upset, I can't bear it."

I hug her again. This time, Anna hugs me back. Then she turns away and enters the house.

I retrace my steps across the yard and back in the direction of the school. Serenity is … missing?

I've heard rumors of people who met with unstable air outside the Community. Last year, Moez wandered the wrong direction in a blizzard and Tomas to the other side of the forest. Both of their bodies were never found. But this is the first time something like this has ever happened *within* the Community boundaries.

Serenity is the same age as Scott and is his play partner when Anna and I are together. She is the sweetest person I know, so gentle. She's slightly taller than Scott but much lighter, like a bulrush.

I close my eyes and see Serenity as she was yesterday before school, her mischievous dark eyes grinning at me under her sun hat, insisting I lug her around the school yard. "Carry me, Katherine," she begged, her arms around my waist.

"Okay, lazybones," I said, with a laugh.

We used to play tag, just the four of us, but not since Serenity picked me to be her human pack mule. She says the heat this summer makes her bushed.

Our favorite game after school used to be swing races. We'd take turns, first Anna and I, and then Scott and Serenity.

Once, when I pushed Serenity, I told her, "I'm sending you to the moon in a rocket. They used to do that, you know."

And Scott said, "Not if Anna sends me there first."

"I've seen the stars move," Serenity told us. "If you watch and don't blink, you can see some of the little ones move in a steady line."

That Serenity is such a monkey, stargazing when she should be in bed, drapes closed.

I gulp. Star monkey ... missing? I hope she is okay.

What happened to Serenity?

I tell myself I have to run back to school or I'll be late. My eyes dart left and right, behind sunflowers and fence posts, searching for Serenity. Maybe she's just behind a tree, napping like a cat. If only ... but the times I venture off the lane to look, she isn't there.

I wipe my sweaty face and catch my breath when I reach the schoolyard.

I think about Anna, Serenity, the note in the cornfield, and Father wanting to see me. My chest tightens, and I feel afraid.

Something is wrong—or am I jumping to a crazy conclusion? Is there a path through my questions that might bring me peace?

Maybe I could make better sense of my thoughts if I weren't always in trouble. I decide to change: from now on, no more questions in front of Brother Michael, Sister Margaret, my parents, or anyone— never again.

The bell rings and I go to my desk. I sit up straight during the Fact Drill on Air Travel and score my usual perfect mark. In Community Service Hour, I efficiently sort out the new brown Winter Uniforms for twenty families, while the other girls only do five. My classmates chatter and laugh; I miss Anna the whole time.

I recite from the Manifesto as if I believed every word.

"We, the last humans on earth, lone survivors of the Ecological Revolution of 1979, hereby bind together, in submission to Father, the eldest and most wise. As the only community in the world, we have become self-sufficient and now live in a sustainable way with our environment. To survive, the human species must pair-bond, work the land, build, and begin new life. We accept the enormity of this task with gratitude and we respect our humble Role on this beautiful but deadly planet."

I take a breath, and then continue.

"Community is everyone, and my questions are irrelevant, as they only serve me. I surrender myself to our collective, and direct my thoughts away from myself—and my selfish need for information—toward what is best for my Community. I accept *surviving together* versus *achieving alone* at the expense of the environment or the basic needs of others. I accept what the earth has to give me and will release myself back into it when my time comes. I strive to live at peace with my surroundings, my people, myself, and to this aim, I pledge my life."

What really happened during the Ecological Revolution? What exactly was it?——

"Father rescued the Brothers and Sisters when they were babies. Father found this perfect place for human civilization to begin again. Father saved our lives and he deserves our respect."

Not just him ... the Uncles and Aunts helped, too. Why is Father's Role in our history more remembered than theirs?

As I continue to recite, I think about Serenity. Could I find out what happened to her? I could fill my secret purple book with my questions and, by writing thoughts down, could figure them out.

But what if there was a Domicile Inspection and my book was found? I decide to hide it in a better place than under my mattress. I want it with me, but this is a problem. The only things that I always carry with me are a wooden writing box and the school stitching and knitting projects I am assigned as homework.

Is my purple book small enough to fit inside my writing box? I decide to check later.

"Individual rule-breakers endanger Community peace and happiness. They must be punished."

"Big improvement today, Katherine," I hear Brother Michael say as I'm dismissed. "I knew you could do it."

Do what? Conform?

I smile to my ears and wave goodbye. It drains all the energy I have left.

Hair flying on the swing
Anna and I are lingering
In the air.

Weightless, falling, soaring high
Happy, giggling, breezing by—
Then we fall.

Looking up to azure sky
I pretend that I can fly.
I am free.

3
Tuesday Afternoon, August 10, 2021

Scott's ear is aching as we walk home from school. He holds his hand to his tilted head as he walks, his eyes brimming with tears. I carry his bag and hold his other hand.

"Almost there," I tell him. My head, my temples, throb as I think of Serenity. Where is she now? Did the boys find her this afternoon?

Dad and Mom are looking at a new kind of low table in the kitchen. Dad is sitting on a stool in front of it, his big knees almost up by his ears; his black hair, wet and matted from his hat. Mom is stroking his tanned neck. They look happy to see us but happy, too, about some secret.

Scott runs over to them and starts to bawl. Mom holds him and waits until he tells her what the matter is.

"My ear hurts," he says. "It really hurts."

Dad gently tousles Scott's hair and looks at me.

"I don't know anything about it," I say. "Scott said it started to ache this afternoon."

"Not another ear infection," Mom says. She looks at Dad, concerned. "I'll need the wagon."

I suck in my breath and look the other way.

"Get ready," she tells me.

Today, I know better than to argue.

I ride on the seat next to Dad while Mom holds Scott, nestled in straw, in the back of the wagon.

I watch Dad's thick-fingered hands as he holds the reins and see cuts, scrapes, gauze wrapped on one finger, and three black nails, likely from the hits of a hammer. I smell him, too—gravy, sweat, sawdust, hay, and, most prominently, lard soap. We are all quiet as we pass the agricultural areas, the school buildings, and the Library. I'm glad that we don't have to talk.

I think about Father. When I was younger, I loved our visits because he would gather me onto his lap for a story. He'd change his voice ten times in the telling and I'd be enthralled. It was with Father I first realized the power of words. A seed was planted in my heart when I was five; I decided that one day I'd write a story, a good one.

On Father's lap, I'd rest my little fingers on his big, soft hands and trace the brown dots, the roads of raised veins, and pull the skin to make it stand up. That always made him laugh, and then I'd smell the garlic sausage or apples on his breath. Once, he showed me a trick and pretended to pop off his finger. When I cried, he hugged me and gave me a piece of honeycomb. At the end of my time, he'd always shine the red light and then visit with Mom, who would be smiling and full of hugs, too.

I was embarrassed, though, when Father told me about the change that every girl goes through to become a woman. When it happened to me, I didn't like how everything seemed different. I think I began to distance myself from Father because of the monthly thing. It's a big nuisance, what with all the rags and the trouble it takes to scrub them clean every night for one week each month, then hang them from the rafters to dry.

The fact that Father is the only one allowed to ask questions irritates me, even though Anna has reminded me it is for medicinal purposes. Also, it's so strange that he's the only one in our Community with the puzzling gadgets—the red light, the gray and silver tubes he uses to hear my heart, to see into my ears. Did Father have his gadgets when he rescued my parents and the other babies from the devastation of the Ecological Revolution? Or did the Uncles and Aunts gather them, as they collected scraps and anything of use, on the way to this settlement? Or maybe the boys created them from that stored collection in the warehouse, from the dismantled cars and trucks that brought all the babies and survivors safe to this location.

Or are these gadgets part of the problem that led to the Ecological Revolution? My teachers say the Individual kept exchanging devices for newer, lighter ones—and this led to enormous environmental waste.

How do Father's gadgets work? Are they powered similarly to the Remote? If so, where does the power come from?

Scott moans as the wagon hits a dip in the dirt road. We pass the residential area where Anna lives but I can't see her house from where I'm sitting. I wonder, is Serenity home yet, maybe playing with the baby or helping to set the table for dinner? Where could she be?

As we approach the Town Circle, I think briefly of Eric, of his parents who clean the teeth of everyone in the Community and distribute the toothbrushes. Will I see him on his way home from searching or haying?

Mom breaks the silence.

"I might ask Father about the Market. It would be so lovely to see the displays of Community talent. If Father saw some of the hidden color, the secret skills of some craftspeople and artisans, I think he would be proud, not sad."

Dad clucks his tongue at the idea. "Caution, Mary. Father has his pace and his reasons. There are issues to think out. The artisans would need materials beyond their rations. The craftspeople would have to donate their creations to the Community because selling the work would offend Father; it would remind him of the Individual and the subsequent Revolution. No, for now the color must stay secret."

Mom ponders this, and then lowers her voice, reaching to touch Dad's back. "Honey, I love my gift. No one else would have thought of hiding a potter's wheel inside a Community low table. Who could have guessed you made it from unused wood from our fuel rations."

Dad looks over his shoulder at Mom and winks. "Somehow I'll get you clay before winter, darling, and we'll rig our stove into a kiln during Snow Break."

I hear my mom's happy exhale as she relaxes against the straw, but my stomach tightens with each click of the horses' hooves on the cobblestone street. Around me, I see buildings packed together and several people milling about before the end of the workday. But no Serenity, and no Eric.

Dad stops the wagon in front of the Main Community Building overlooking the Town Circle and helps Mom and Scott off the end of the wagon bed.

"I might as well wait here," he tells us.

Mom nods and helps Scott up the rock steps and into the stone and brick building. I follow them. I'm hoping Father will only have time to see Scott. We enter the room with the sign, *Dr. White, Community Doctor* on it and I am disappointed. There is only one other person waiting, a woman named Della. Her twins were the first grandchildren to be born in the Community—quite a milestone to celebrate. Another woman at the desk, whose name I forget—Ellen? Eileen?—speaks with Mom while Scott and I find a seat.

"You're being brave," I tell him.

"It hurts," he says, loudly.

I pat his hand. "I know. Think about something else."

He is quiet for a moment. "Can they see out?"

I have no idea what Scott is talking about but I know that Della is listening. I take control of the conversation.

"We can all see out of the windows."

"No. Can the puppets and the people on Remote see out? Into our house?"

Della clicks her tongue in disapproval and stares at me.

My cheeks go red. "You know what your teachers in Level Two say about questions."

Scott looks confused. "But we always—"

I kiss him on the forehead to interrupt him. "We always listen to the Brothers and Sisters. Now, no more talking—you're tired."

I pat his head and reach for the knitting homework in my bag as Mom returns.

She leans over to me. "About fifteen minutes. We can all go in together."

Father's office has a table on which we must sit during our visits, a cabinet with vials and bowls, several cupboards, and three chairs.

There is also a second door, likely leading to a closet, and an open window behind his desk. Fresh air from the alley blows the half-drawn drapes, and Father's papers rustle under his collection of rock paper weights. Anna and I found the rust-colored one when digging by the lakeside years ago. To brighten up the walls, Father has collected pictures from children, including one I drew in pen—a view of the horizon from my bedroom window. I could draw well when I was a little kid. I wonder why I stopped. Was it because I learned to read novels?

The room is clean and brightened by afternoon sun, making the sunflower-oil lamp unnecessary.

Father is sitting at his desk when we come in. He is hunched over a pile of papers, his elbows on his desktop and his hands spread through his thick, white hair. Is he worried about Serenity? Is he upset from his meeting with Anna's family?

He looks up at us, tries to smile, then moves around the desk, holding his arms out for Scott.

"Here you are," he says, lifting my brother to a hug. "Such a big man."

"I lost another tooth last week," Scott tells him, "but my ear hurts today."

"Let's fix it all up then," Father tells him, looking at Mom and me. "Please, have a seat."

Today Father looks older—if that's even possible—than how I remember him from a few months ago. He is wearing the brown and beige summer uniform of a non-laboring male, and I never noticed it before, but there is a wrinkle where his ears meet his face. The lines on his forehead are deep and look like spring planting rows.

We sit in the chairs provided, and Father helps Scott onto the table.

"It's good you came together so I can visit with all three of you."

I look at Mom, but she is staring straight ahead.

Father looks into Scott's ear with a metal instrument. My brother squirms and makes a face.

"Another ear infection," he says to Mom.

"So many," Mom almost whispers.

"Common for children his age," Father tells her.

Still, I see his shoulders drop as he pulls vials, fluffy wool, and other ingredients from his cabinets. Is he tired or worried? I've only ever seen Father calm or happy.

He mixes a few drops of this and that into a bowl, gets Scott to lie down, and drops some of the mixture into Scott's ear. He seals the ear with the fluffy wool and hands a tiny, brown glass bottle with a rubber top to Mom.

"One dropper, half-full, twice a day, for five days after the symptoms disappear."

"Thank you, Father," Mom says in her mouse-voice, as Scott climbs off the table and back onto her lap.

Why is Mom so quiet right now with Father?

Dr. White moves to prepare something else—this time a syringe.

My hands grip my skirt. My chest tightens. Is that for me? What's wrong with me?

I look over at Mom. She has tears behind her lashes. Is she afraid for me?

Father tells Mom that he would like to speak to me alone. *Don't leave!*

"Of course," she whispers. She takes Scott back into the waiting room as Father closes the door.

"Onto the table, please," Father tells me.

I obey. Father reaches into the cabinet for another instrument. "Look straight ahead," he says.

The instrument shines a red light into my eyes.

"Good." He puts away the red light and writes something in pencil on the pile of papers on his desk.

Then he sits in one of the chairs, sighing as he does. "Katherine, have you been in trouble at home, lately? No Remote?"

I stare at him. How does he know?

He continues. "Your teachers mentioned you in their school up-date."

He knows everything!

"We have such hopes for you. Some Community Leaders wonder if we have overestimated your potential. Perhaps you are only capable of manual labor."

I swallow my questions and stare at his newly polished shoes.

"Quite like your dad," he says, then pauses.

In what way? Perhaps Dad asked a lot of questions, too.

"School was quite challenging for him, as I remember it."

But I don't have difficulty in school! School is easy. Is the only thing that matters that I don't ask questions? Doesn't all my ten years of high achievement factor at all?

"Only two weeks until Harvest Break, and then, at the end of October, the new Roles will be assigned, based on merit. And by merit, I mean a consistent demonstration of respect to your Brothers and Sisters."

I gulp. He's not telling me it's too late. Or is he?

"You can't afford any more breaks of obedience to the Manifesto—or else it's off to the field you go. Do you have any questions?"

It's a test. I know it.

"No, Father. Sorry, Father."

He shows his yellow, worn teeth—a kind of half-smile—and goes back to his desk. "Please get your mother and stay in the waiting room with Scott."

Relieved, I glance over at the syringe as I slide off the table. I walk to where Scott is waiting, dozy.

Mom walks past me but she doesn't make eye contact.

Is the syringe for Mom? What's wrong with her?

The door closes and I sit on the edge of my chair, listening, waiting. The only sound I hear is Scott's slight breathing.

How does Father know that I haven't been watching the Remote? Why did Father tell me that I am like Dad?

As I wait, I fiddle with my writing box. I pull out my ink and writing utensils so I can examine the bottom.

Could I find a way to hide my purple book in here? There wouldn't be much room, but I could cut off the edges to make it fit.

I hear someone turning the doorknob and I fumble to put my stuff away in time. Mom comes out of Father's office. She has been crying.

This morning
While I'm churning cream
Scott drags himself
Downstairs
Carrying the heat stones from our beds.
Carefully
One at a time
He sets them by the stove.
Scream of pain—
We all run over
Burn on the wrist
Tears everywhere
Frantic
Searching for cold water
And relief.
A long time passes
Until cries melt to whimpers
And Scott finds comfort
In bread and new butter.

4
Tuesday Evening, August 10, 2021

Without explanation, Mom walks straight out of the waiting room. I nudge Scott awake and collect our things. He is disoriented and wonders where we are.

"Father's office," I tell him. "It's time to go."

"Where's Mom?"

Scott always wakes up slowly.

"She's out with Dad, I guess."

I am right. We find them outside, hugging by the horses. We watch. It is an awkward moment of quiet. I look up at the late afternoon sky.

What's going on? How can they talk without words? And then I understand. What's going on between them has happened before. That's why Mom doesn't talk and Dad doesn't fish around for an answer.

What happened in Father's office, with the syringe?

After a long minute, Dad lifts Scott onto the back of the wagon and motions for me to sit with him there. Then he helps Mom up onto the wagon seat and grips the reins.

I watch them, looking for clues, anything.

Mom stares straight ahead, her back straight until we leave the Town Circle. Scott leans against me and closes his eyes.

When the buildings are behind us, Mom starts to cry again. Her sniffles turn into louder sobs. Scott shifts. Dad puts his arm around Mom and pulls her to him, their heads together in quiet whisperings.

What can I do?

Scott stirs again, this time waking. I hold him tight and whisper into his uncovered ear.

"Go back to sleep. There's still a while to go."

His head rests against me. I'm not sure whether he is sleeping or thinking. I wonder if he is upset, as I am, by Mom's weeping. I relax my body against the side of the wagon and gaze at the emerging display of color on the horizon, without really appreciating it. I must find out what is happening to Mom—and what happened to Serenity. Even if she's been found, it's upsetting that she was ever lost.

I know that, in the last day, Anna has lost more than her sister. I can't remember when I first knew that the Community wasn't perfect. I guess it was when Mom told me about the four babies she miscarried between Scott and me. I lost something the day I learned that sometimes babies die.

Scott fiddles with some twine on the wagon floor, in amongst the straw. I stroke his blond hair and tuck it behind his ear. He sits up.

"What's wrong with Mom?" he says in a loud whisper.

"I don't know."

For a while we are quiet, as if dumb.

"It's my fault," he says, his lower lip quivering, his voice almost drowned by the wagon and horse sounds.

"No, no," I say, pulling him back to me.

"If I hadn't got a sore ear, this wouldn't have happened."

I try to reassure him with the truth. "Mom's tears have nothing to do with you."

"But she wasn't crying before my appointment. She was happy about the low table."

Only one fact will alleviate my brother's guilt, but I have mixed feelings about sharing it. Without fully thinking it through, I blurt it out. "Mom had an appointment with Father after I did, while you were sleeping."

"Then Father made her cry. I hate Father," he says, under his breath. "He's bad."

What a shocking thought. Father, who deserves our respect, is bad? As I think this, I realize the influence I have over Scott. In some ways, I'm almost his third parent. I have to protect him. He doesn't know how to live with contradictions, as I assume other people do, as I must learn to. I speak into his uncovered ear. "You don't hate Father; he made your ear stop hurting."

I watch his face as he remembers this.

"Sometimes Brothers and Sisters have problems Father can't fix." I wait a moment, and then continue. "You enjoy Father's red light."

Scott nods, with some reluctance.

"And he has the neatest instruments."

His face lifts and he smiles, relieved.

"See, you're not angry with Father. You're just upset that Mom is sad. I am, too. We'll help her and give her lots of love until she's better."

Scott hugs me tightly, but I am a storm in turmoil. Scott must feel my tension because he pulls away from me. He fiddles with a small, thin, flat piece of wood lying on the wagon floor, under the straw. In my frustration, I take it from him and rip bits off the sides, chucking them over the edge.

Then I realize what I have in my hands: this piece of wood is small enough to fit as a false bottom into my writing box. My purple book could go underneath. I try to imagine this but Scott interrupts my thoughts.

"Why does Father look different from other men?"

"He's old," I say, tucking the wood piece into my book bag.

His reply is quick. "Why aren't there other old people in the Community?"

He has my attention now. If I tell him about the older Uncles and Aunts who died, it will only lead to more questions.

I know the responsible thing to do. I decide to let his teachers tell him about the Ecological Revolution and put an end to his probing.

"Questions are a rude and elementary way of seeking information."

"But we always—" he says, loud enough to make Dad turn around.

I remember our discussion in Father's waiting room and the disapproving, eavesdropping Della, who clicked her tongue at us. Scott is too young to understand.

"I was wrong. I'm not going to use questions anymore. It's important that we listen to the Brothers and Sisters. They know best."

Scott moves to the other side of the wagon and sticks out his lower lip. I let him pout for a few minutes, but then he forgets and starts to toss straw bits from the wagon bed over the side. I stare at the horizon, at the sunset, and shift my seating position from one numb cheek to the other. I try to count the numbers of pinks and oranges before the scene changes again.

Tonight, I get why Dad loves dawn. The colors make me feel less alone, as if maybe the sky isn't so dangerous, as if maybe someone is bigger than me, bigger than Father, and completely in control of this recovering, war-torn planet. Maybe there is a Planet Keeper out there past the Community boundary.

And perhaps color doesn't mean selfish individualism. Maybe color is just beauty that is shared, beauty that imitates nature.

Maybe I'm not supposed to think like this ... but there are always words in my head, words that make me want to describe things and tell stories. I get a delicious idea. Will Father someday create the Role of Storyteller for the Community? Maybe the Storyteller could tell bedtime stories through the Remote each night.

The farmhouse comes into view. Scott and I watch as our parents get down from the wagon. Mom takes trembling baby steps into the house. Dad instructs us, his eyes on her.

"Take care of the animals, fix yourselves some dinner, then wash up and go to bed. Extra chores for you both tonight."

We nod.

"And shut the drapes, too," he says, running to open the door for Mom.

I know. They keep the light and heat from going out the windows. But why is that so important in the summer? It's not as if anyone in the field is looking through our windows, right?

Scott jumps off the wagon but I crawl down. My foot has fallen asleep. I shake it out and grab the reins.

Although these horses belong to the Community, Scott has

named them: Trotter and Pitch. He talks to them while I unhitch the wagon. All these tools in the barn came with the field, which Dad received when he got his Role. Dad was twenty at the time, though I will only be fifteen when it's my turn. Over the years, Father has decided that although school is important, contributing to the Community is more so.

Anna hopes to get a Role with the Level Ones. She loves to invent games to play with her younger brothers and sisters. If we both get Roles near the school, we might ask if we can share a home … that is, before Eric and I … My face reddens. Why does my mind always dash instead of dally?

Father chose Mom to marry my dad. It was a happy coincidence, Mom says, because they always liked each other but were too shy to let the other know. There have been some free-choice marriages in the Community, but they only happen when the man and woman are younger than seventeen—that's the age when Father matches couples. If a couple pairs earlier, they are encouraged to marry quickly, and can do so anytime after they are given their Life Roles.

Anna's parents laugh a lot together. That's what I always notice every time I visit her home. If I had to marry someone that I didn't love, I hope at least we could enjoy each other's company. Does love ever grow from friendship or does it have to be there at the start?

Aside from Eric, the boys in my level are very immature, always playing tricks on each other or teasing the girls. How will the girls in my level ever find husbands amongst them? How long will it take before I know if Eric is right for me? How did Father choose so perfectly for my mom and dad?

Dad keeps the tools in excellent condition and well-ordered, not just because of monthly Farm Inspections, but also because he can be a perfectionist who values doing things right. I can be like that, too. Maybe there are some other ways I'm similar to Dad.

I light the lantern, take the bit out Pitch's mouth, then hand Scott a pitchfork.

"We have to help the horses and feed all the animals now," I tell him. "You make sure there's enough straw in the stalls."

Pitch is much taller that Trotter, so I stand on a crate to brush his back. It makes me wonder: were Pitch's distant descendants warhorses? What did they see of the world? Pitch jerks his head back, exhaling steamy horse breath. I climb on his back to smooth out his mane. This makes me think of Anna's black hair, which makes me think of Serenity. I blink tears and wipe my nose on my sleeve. Where could she be? Could she have run away? Tonight, as I'm grooming Pitch, I do something for the very first time. I ask the Planet Keeper, if He exists, to keep Serenity safe, wherever she is. It makes me feel better, as if I've delegated my worry to someone else.

Then it's Trotter's turn, and I think about the note and Mom, then Eric for a sweet second, then back to Serenity.

Scott finishes with the straw, so I scoop out grain and hay portions for the horses and direct him to do the evening routine for the animals that have been rationed to us for the year: twenty chickens, our dairy cows (Peat and her not-so-small calf), one pig with two piglets. I finish Trotter's grooming and put blankets on both of the horses, leading them to their meals in the stalls.

I turn down the lantern and we hurry to the kitchen while it's still twilight.

Ever since I was young, I have loved this kitchen—the big stove in the center, its pipe leading up through the open ceiling, past the upstairs loft. The plan for this old house is perfect for hanging clothes to dry off the rails upstairs in the winter and heating the second floor with the warm air that rises.

But today, the kitchen seems forlorn and empty. I stock a mixture of coal, peat, and wood from the fuel shed, which I will add into the stove's belly throughout the evening.

The Remote comes on then, and Scott pulls the kitchen stool to the alcove behind the pantry where he watches it.

On the pantry shelves are my family's portions of canned Community vegetables, fruits, meats, and fish. There is a basket of eggs, some bins of flour, and many kinds of dried herbs and plants labeled in jars. In the icebox, there's a wedge of this morning's bread, Peat's milk, some cheese and butter. Scott and I don't need anything special tonight so I just pull out the contents of the icebox. Judging by the size of the ice block, it was delivered recently, probably when we were at Father's office.

I see some uncooked, peeled potatoes in the kitchen basin; I decide to boil these, too. I pump enough water for two large pots to do our washing-up and put a smaller pot on the stove for the potatoes. Finally, I fill the kettle, just in case it's needed. In the cast-iron pan, I lay two slices of rye bread, butter side down, with slivers of cheese on top.

I will ask my parents if there's anything I can bring them. I knock timidly on their door, not because I am shy but because I am eager to be of help tonight.

"Come in," Dad says,

Mom is lying in bed. Dad gets up from the chair as I enter.

"The animals are taken care of and the water is on to boil."

Mom smiles with her mouth but not her eyes. "Thank you, Katherine." Her face is red and streaked from more crying. I try to read her eyes to find out what is the matter. I know I can't ask, though I feel I desperately need to know. Would making a comment about her tears be seeking information that doesn't belong to me? Will Mom tell me why she is crying when she thinks I need to know? What if that time never comes?

"I'll make mint tea and boiled potatoes."

Mom shakes her head. Dad answers.

"We're not hungry. Maybe just tea."

Mom agrees with a nod.

As I leave, Dad adds, "Let's all make it an early night tonight."

I know what he means. Scott and I must be in bed within the hour. I close the door behind me.

From downstairs, I hear Scott call out, "The red light. Katherine, come quick."

I take my time on the stairs. I don't care tonight.

"You missed it," Scott grumbles. He is sitting close to the box, too close.

I put the melted cheese bread onto a plate and pour him a cup of milk.

"It's just the Community Report," Scott says, "but come sit with me."

I get my bread and milk, too, and join him. Father is speaking through the Remote, only his head and shoulders visible. He looks at us while he reads what must be a memorized speech, because he doesn't break eye contact.

"The Community extends its gratitude to Brother Joel and Brother Shawn for their efficient ice delivery today, and for their terrific management of the ice supply, which looks likely to last the summer. The Community praises Sister Mae and Brother Caleb for having completed their Residential winterizing preparations before anyone else in the whole Community. The Community encourages Brother Edward, Brother Philip, Brother Jake, and Sister Leah to not be among the last, as they have been for the past two years. The Community praises Thomas and his Level Ten son, Gerald, for volunteering to fix the school slide."

Ha! Who other than Gerald to fix it? He broke it.

"Harvest storage bins have been swept and prepared. First frost still seems several weeks away. Lake travel restrictions are firm until after Harvest is collected. Cannery focus to switch from fish and preserves to tomatoes. Residential volunteers needed to come forward to collect and store the mature dried-peat harvest. The Community looks on track to recover from last year's canola harvest's poor yield and the entire barley crop failure.

"The weather tomorrow is expected to reach highs of twenty-seven, lows of fourteen, no possibility of precipitation, and light dew. Haying must continue as this week's priority, with labor requested from the Senior boys. Wheat fields reported ready to straight cut requesting forestry workers to aid, starting at the northeast corner. Twelve percent of the barley crop is swathed, and we continue to request fishing labor to continue tomorrow. All members are expected to volunteer during free time until the Harvest is safely gathered."

The kettle hoots and I get up to prepare the tea. The potatoes are starting to boil but won't be ready for a while. I wish, again, that there was something more I could do for Mom. If only I knew what happened to her.

Some clue is probably in Father's office, in that stack of papers he was leaning on when we first came in. Perhaps he has recorded what happened in Mom's appointment. But to steal in and trespass in Father's office? I filter the idea out of my head. I could never do that; it would be too rude, too irreverent. And what if I got caught? I wish I could just ask Mom.

The temperature of the washing-up water is warm enough. I bring the tea to my parents and ask Dad to help me siphon the heated water to the washing room. I find my parents already in their nightclothes, and Dad gets up to help me without my needing to ask.

Mom and Dad take turns in the washing room while I mash the potatoes.

Scott goes in then, and I meet him there, pushing his head forward above the basin so the warm water runs from his neck, over his head, and across his face. I scrub at the back of his neck, wipe under his arms, and bring the basin low to wash his feet. Then I dry them both and brush his teeth.

"Be careful with my loose tooth," Scott tells me.

Then it's my turn—the water is only lukewarm, and not much of it is left. The water on my neck wets only some of my long hair, but my face feels refreshed anyway. I reflect on the day—sneaking to see Anna, the visit to Father, Mom crying. My head is full, my body tired. But I need to write to make it all real, so then I can make it go away.

In my room, I open my purple book and start:

August 10, 2021

Serenity has been lost for almost one full day, nineteen hours. And if she hasn't been found, she's about to spend her first full night alone.

I stare at those words, willing them to be a made-up story. Wiping tears, I tell myself that she's probably found. But maybe she's— no! I won't think this way.

When I was younger, the Community was perfect. Now all I hear in my head are questions. When I don't speak them, it's as if I have two voices: the one that is allowed to talk and the one that must be slowly extinguished. Do other people in the Community just have one voice? When they aren't talking, do they have thoughts inside that want to speak? Am I crazy? Am I slowly dying?

I think back to the note in the cornfield. Whoever wrote it said that they saw the outside come, through the sky. Is it possible that other life exists on this planet? Wouldn't that be a good thing for the Community to find? Wouldn't that be encouraging to know: that the planet is beginning to heal? Could this even be true?

There might be kids in the Outside World. Are they similar to Anna, to me?

But what if this is all there is? What Role will I have in the Community? Would my Role be sweeter if Eric were with me? Will I ever know?

In my dreams, I think I hear a wail, a man scream in anguish at the moon out near the outhouse. Frightened, I awake, and I lie in bed, frozen, listening. But I must be wrong. My worry is making me think crazy things.

I wonder what a birthday would feel like.
I'll pretend Anna's birthday is tomorrow.
I will make her a molasses cake with honey icing.
I'll stitch her name in colored thread—yellow—on a kerchief,
The color of daffodils, soon to poke their brave heads through the snow.
Daffodils remind me of Anna: strong and hope-filled.
Father would not approve.
"A birthday is a celebration of the Individual."
But I'm sure Father never had a best friend like Anna.
Anna is worth celebrating.

5

Wednesday Morning, August 11, 2021

Anna is away again. I look around the room while I wait for Brother Michael and Sister Margaret to start our Fact Drill. Eugenia and Prudence whisper and look back in my direction. I sharpen my pencil, then see them coming towards me.

What do they want? I yawn and smooth my skirt. When they are standing above me, I look up.

"Uh … hello," I say, as if surprised.

"Hello, *Kath*erine," Eugenia says, emphasizing the first syllable of my name. Prudence giggles. Prudence always giggles. It's why the boys like her best. She'll be married by Spring Planting, for sure.

"You're alone today," Eugenia observes, prying about Anna's business.

"You're very perceptive," I tell her. "It's a good skill to have in your Life Role of a …" I think for a second, "Seed Separator."

Emily, in the seat ahead of me, pops a laugh.

But Prudence drops her jaw.

Eugenia's smile stays frozen. "How helpful to have parents in manual labor, so you can ask them for help—that is, if they can spare their five minutes of free time."

I don't blink. "We'll see who is pulling weeds next spring, and who is—" I almost blurt out my desired Role but then she interrupts me.

"So you and Eric ..." Eugenia says, emphasizing each word.

I suck in my breath.

"Told you," Eugenia says, looking at Prudence, a smirk on her face. Eugenia looks back at me then, with the cold eyes of a raptor bird. "Well, I'm sure you know he wants to be with a girl who gets a good Role. His parents *insist* on it, too."

What would it take for this girl to be content with observing her own life? If she did, she'd be top of the class and not second to me.

Then Eugenia adds, "Anna is never away. Must be serious."

"I heard something about Anna's sister, too," Prudence tells me.

I can't stand to hear anymore. I point to the front of the room where Brother Michael is gathering papers off his desk.

I watch them go, blinking back tears. So *Serenity has not been found.* If she was, Anna would be here, and Prudence and Eugenia would be telling me that the boys found Serenity yesterday.

And now the gossips know about Eric and me. Did they see us in the schoolyard yesterday? Is our relationship, if we are to grow one, strong enough to survive spite from those human Cowbirds? Anna would like that term for Eugenia and Prudence, too. I must remember to tell her. Will another search party look for Serenity again today?

Brother Michael is at the lectern, laying out his notes. He cracks his knuckles and smoothes the wrinkled pants on his slim legs. His coarse black hair, cut short, always pokes up in the back of his head, despite the many times I've seen him attempt to flatten it. There's a small brown mole on his left cheek but I think it suits his young face. His nails are always clean and clipped short, his eyebrows neat, and his skin is like the creamy neck of a deer.

Then he speaks in his clear, calm tone. "After lunch, we'll be reading in the Library to the Level One girls. Sister Millie has selected several books for us to share with them. Tomorrow, our focus will go entirely to Home Skills with an emphasis on botulism, preparing poultices, and other aspects of pre-nursing. For Dictation today, we'll focus on features of Community Government."

We grab our pencils. Brother Michael pauses, and then begins.

"Fact. Since the beginning of time, humans have been obsessed with the idea of a perfect world. Although we are the only humans alive on the planet, we can benefit from the mistakes of past civilizations. We can learn from their disasters. We can correct what they did wrong; we can achieve perfection."

If perfection is possible, why do I keep making mistakes? Can a perfect Community exist if I am, at my core, imperfect?

"Fact. A perfect society is one without any blemishes—money, ownership, materialism, greed, hunger, genetic imperfection, physical or mental abnormalities, pollution, or crime. In a perfect society, there is cooperation, accountability, community, and pride in corporate—not Individual—accomplishments. In a perfect society, people treat each other with respect. They do not ask questions or assume rights to information that does not belong to them. To continue to question is to hold onto a spirit of innovation and individuality—the two main contributors to the Ecological Revolution."

I look up at Brother Michael. His eyes are shining and his hands punctuate his message. He really believes this. What does he know that I don't?

"Fact. Father is the only person in the Community to remember the horrors—which can never be described, in order to protect your innocence—of the Ecological Revolution and the devastation that followed. Father, alone, carries these heavy memories and deserves your respect, reverence, and obedience.

"Fact. Father assumes leadership of the Community, but he delegates responsibilities to certain leaders, who collect information and report back to him. They stay anonymous to everyone—even their families—and are able to effect changes in the Community by leading from within, rather than out in front.

"Fact. Father and his chosen Community Leaders decide on guidelines and rules for the entire Community in confidential meetings."

Brother Michael continues on until our Community Service Hour. We are needed in the Dairy, where we go once a week to help with a variety of jobs associated with making cheese. It's a fifteen-minute walk, but often we have to run when Brother Michael or Sister Margaret talk too long and time is short.

Today is one of those times, and I jog at the front of my class to avoid the Cowbird girls. It's a hot day to run, and we arrive sweaty and red-faced, taking turns to gulp cool water from the pump.

The Dairy has prepared a huge amount of newly clabbered milk that will be made into cheese. Our Level helps cut cheesecloth, but our primary duty today is to wash pots, spoons, colanders, and compressors in hot, sterile water. I perspire in the steam rising from the deep sinks.

Sister Bernie inspects every step of this process. She always reminds me of a hen, the way her head bobs as she flutters around to organize us. And her nose is her beak. Once I told Anna this and she clucked around like a chicken while Sister Bernie was in the other room. I almost laugh, just thinking of this.

"Careful, girls," Sister Bernie repeats. "If it's not perfectly clean, the cheese will spoil."

I notice her strawberry hands are peeling and her curly black hair is pulled tight at her white temples with a hairnet.

My own hands are swollen red from the hot water, but they return to shape as we walk back to the school. I hope my Role isn't working in the Dairy, though I know for one of us it will have to be.

During lunch, I sit under a tree reading a book about the *Titanic*, an ocean liner that sank in 1912, more than one hundred years ago. Only the rich people were allowed in the lifeboats and the poor people were locked in their cabins to drown.

Often, after reading a history book, I feel torn. I am alive when so many others have died. I feel some relief at that, but sometimes guilt and frustration, too. The book is over and I still have so many questions. Could human beings really treat each other this way— over money? Why do people need money, anyway? Why wouldn't there be enough lifeboat rations for everyone? Why would all these people waste their fuel rations to cross the ocean? And how did the sunken ship damage the ocean ecosystem?

I close the book and swat at some flies that buzz too close. I wonder about Serenity, if a different search party is looking for her now that the boys must cut hay. And I wonder about Mom, though she seemed stronger this morning. I think she enjoyed the bread I made, though I know I overcooked it. The bell rings and I walk to the Library to meet the Level Ones.

I find my partner, Misha, watching for me from the door. She runs for a hug and I carry her into the library, her freckled pip of a nose almost touching mine. Hidden under her primary cap is an orange mop of ringlets, blonde lashes, and green eyes the color of sweet-pea pods.

"We have a surprise," she tells me.

The younger girls line up in rows, then, and crouch into tiny balls on the wood floor. A few sunhats roll off, are retrieved, and the girls titter and wait for their cue.

Hyacinth, another Level One, recites "Ode to a Sunflower."

The giggly girls begin to unfurl and reach up to the roof.

> *"Seed along the lanes*
> *Watch it grow, grow, grow*
> *Chop off the heads*
> *Pulp the fiber; make the paper*
> *Press the seed, extract the oil,*
> *And feed the rest to the an-ni-mals."*

We clap for the group and give polite smiles. Then Misha examines today's book choices while I find a quiet corner near the Library Office.

Maybe this will be my office. Will I get a chance to work with books like Sister Millie, too?

Misha comes back and places the book, *Susan's Pet Mouse*, into my lap. I lift the worn cover and read the title. Misha points to the picture at the bottom of the page and smiles. I start to read.

Susan lives in the Residential Area with her parents and her sister.

Susan's dad is Brother Thomas, the Community Shearer.

Misha leans against my arm and begins to suck her thumb.

One day, Susan was helping to move hay in the barn when she saw a baby mouse. The mouse was so young that its eyes were still shut.

"Oh," said Susan. "I should help this baby mouse. It has lost its mom."

I stop reading as Sister Millie passes. She bends down to greet us, her blonde hair draping across her slim shoulders like a shawl. Misha hastily pulls her thumb from her mouth and buries her hand into her lap.

Sister Millie laughs and pats Misha on the head. "Oh, you're a cute one," she says, her blue eyes twinkling. "I see you're reading *Susan's Pet Mouse*."

"Yes," says Misha. "My favorite."

"I got the idea for the story from Katherine, here," she tells Misha.

I look at Sister Millie, my mouth open, and almost say, "You did?" The librarian writes books, also? I didn't know that. Wouldn't it be wonderful if … If only …

Sister Millie laughs again. "You were always adopting stray animals when you were younger. Your mom and I thought it was so adorable; I just had to try to capture a character like you in my story. And that's not the only time I did, either."

"I didn't know you write, too," I tell Sister Millie.

"Well, we can't claim authorship on books," she says simply. "It would take the focus off the Community and put it onto one individual. After all, a farmer can't stamp his name on his timothy, brom, or flax harvests. His efforts are for the good of all."

I want to hear more, but Misha is pulling my arm, begging me to read on.

Sister Millie winks at me, then stands to address the others.

"Girls, your attention here, please. When you're finished your book, assist your younger partner to draw a picture of our school mascot, the Canada Goose. Please also write some descriptive words or phrases about the birds. For example, they pair-mate for life, are excellent parents, are respectful of older birds, and have beauty in their uniformity."

"It's for the Life Roles assembly," Misha tells me. "Room One is doing something special for the Seniors in Room Three."

"That's lovely," I tell Misha, though my tummy tightens at the thought of the upcoming ceremony.

"Read," Misha begs, and I continue:

> Susan put the mouse into her apron pocket. "Maybe I will find its mom," said Susan. She looked behind the hay bales and the woodpile but the mom was not there. She looked behind the door and beside the stable but there was no—

Out of the corner of my eye, I see that Father has walked past us and is talking with Sister Millie in her office.

I keep reading even though I freeze up inside. My face feels hot again, as if I just ran, and I hold my breath while Misha studies the black and white pictures. I remember my appointment yesterday. What is Father doing here? What happened to Mom yesterday? What important business would bring Father to the Library? I catch my breath. Perhaps he's found Serenity?

Sister Millie and Father whisper words I can't hear. Father opens a leather bag and pulls out some papers, which he shows to Sister Millie.

Misha has noticed my disinterest in our book. She sighs—loudly. Scott does this, too, whenever I read to him without effort. I add expression to keep Misha satisfied, but try to keep an ear tuned to the office.

> That night during supper, Susan asked her mom what baby mice like to eat.
>
> "Susan," said her mom, "you are too old to ask questions."
>
> Susan thought, I must find out what to feed my mouse, or it will starve. She tried again. "Mom, I think baby mice must need to eat bread," said Susan.
>
> "No," said her mom. "Baby mice are mammals. They drink their mom's milk."

I am aware that Father and Sister Millie are no longer talking. I look up and see them smiling over a piece of paper. I finish the book just as Father packs up his papers and Sister Millie walks back into the Library. As Father closes his bag, a paper falls onto the floor but he doesn't notice.

"Get paper and pencils for the goose drawing," I tell Misha.

She gets up slowly, still looking at the picture on the back cover. "It's a good story," she says, mostly to herself.

Father walks past me through the Library. I look into the office and see that the paper is still on the floor. My heart beats faster. He left it behind. Should I pick it up? Should I tell Sister Millie that he forgot it?

She is at one side of the Library, handing out brown crayons, but the paper is ten feet from where I am sitting. I move quietly to the office and, without really deciding to and before I think it through, I'm looking at the paper on the floor.

The paper is beautiful, thin, smooth, and fine. At the top of the letter is a rich, golden stamp and a word: *Canada*.

I skim further down the page.

Horace,

Father has a name?

> *to inform you ... legislation ... Armed Forces ... Full funding anticipated ... not guaranteed until Monday ... The office is running smoothly ... anticipate upcoming report ... from all departments next week ... I remain with you in support and ...*
> > *Ruth*

Who is Ruth? What does this letter mean?

I jump at a sound behind me and turn around. Father is there! And Sister Millie behind him, her mouth open, her face horrified.

My face flushes hot and I gulp to catch my breath. I drop the paper and try to stand.

How did he come back? He was gone. I thought he left.

"You dropped this," I say, stammering. I kneel to pick up the paper again but my trembling hands struggle with this simple task.

"You read it," Father says, a muscle in his jaw tightening.

"You left this behind. I saw it drop from your bag. I came to pick it up for you, to give to Sister—"

"No," Father says, shaking his head, his eyes sad. "You force my hand, Katherine," he says with a deep sigh. "Administer the second warning," he tells Sister Millie.

She gulps then and nods slowly. "This is rare, very unexpected."

Second warning? When was my first warning?

"Yes," says Father, rubbing his forehead, then his eyes. "And very disappointing. Cut her hair."

I gasp. My hair? I place my hand at the back of my neck and breathe faster. "No, please. I'm so sorry. I'll never do it again. I beg you."

Father turns to Sister Millie. "You'll have to write a report. I'll need a copy, as will her teachers and parents."

I can't breathe. I'll be the only girl in school with short hair. Everyone in the Community will know. Will they ever forget? Is it all over for me now?

Father bends over to pick the paper off the floor.

"Please," I whisper, wiping my eyes. "I didn't understand. It was just words. I didn't even realize I was reading it."

"I wish you would trust me," Father says, touching my face with his hand before he leaves the library.

Sister Millie leads me by the elbow, from the office to join the others.

"Gather round," she calls to the group, her voice unsteady. The other girls surround us but Sister Millie excuses herself for a moment. She returns from her office with a kerchief and scissors. I bite my lip. I'd weep except that Eugenia looks triumphant.

Sister Millie wipes her eyes and blows her nose. Then she says, "Katherine read Father's private paper. I wonder if the Level Ones know what private means."

They all nod like spring-necked wooden dolls, the younger ones so sweet in their obvious sincerity.

I look at the floor. Misha is there, by my feet, looking up at me like a lost mouse. Why do I have to be punished in front of her?

I stare straight ahead at the faded, beige poster on the wall: *Pursue Perfection. It is Possible.*

"Well, Katherine knew what that meant, but she did a terrible thing. She disobeyed an essential part of the Manifesto. She did not reverence Father. She hunted information that did not belong to her. And we know what happens then …"

I take a deep breath.

"Those who break Community Rules must be punished," recite fifty feminine voices.

"That's right."

Behind me I hear a clink of metal. Snip. I feel my hair fall away as it releases from my head, the weight of it cut free, the horrid lightness—nakedness—at my neck. My peripheral vision catches Sister Millie, holding up the length of it to show the others.

"Look! Look at this lovely, long, honey-brown hair that Katherine has lost, all because she was too stubborn to respect Father. And now, every time you see her, you must remember what happens to those who disobey the Manifesto."

Sister Millie taps me gently on the shoulder and I know what is expected of me.

"I'm sorry," I say, swallowing salty thickness in my throat. My heart beats up near my ears and I wish the floorboards would open so I could crawl away. They don't and I close my eyes. The two groups are then dismissed to return to the Girls' Building.

"It's very disappointing," Sister Millie tells them as they leave, "but the goose project must be postponed."

I stand there until I think that everyone has left, and then a single, hot tear leads a flood of tears down along my nose. I brush them away and feel my neck. This sign of my lovely femininity, my maturity, is gone, and now my hair barely covers my ears. I am nothing but an ugly spectacle now.

Sister Millie writes the letters of report. When her pen drops, I reach out for the papers and turn to leave, but she steps in front of me and takes my head into her hands. There are tears in her eyes, too, and I smell rose petals on her wrists.

"Katherine, you can recover. A search for answers is a vain quest from which no one ever returns. However, there is hope. Meditation can help you. Every morning and every night—do it. Simply quiet your heart and empty your mind. Release *yourself*—all your questions and inquisitiveness—and breath in an acceptance of *us*, the good of the Community, as your *Center*."

"I'll try," I say, averting my eyes, and Sister Millie releases her grip so I can step away.

She catches my hand as I pass by, and gives it a kind squeeze.

Behind a tree, I continue to weep. My Life Role is decided now. Even working in the Dairy will be too good for me. I'll never be able to make books, never be able to write. And how many years must pass before I even look like the other girls? Will Eric choose me still when he learns about this? The tears fall again when I remember what might never be—something sweet to my lips—and a rolling sadness blankets my chest.

It seems the outside air cannot cool my hot face no matter how long I wait.

Should I just go home? Would that earn me a third warning? What would happen then?

I walk to the Girls' Building, returning to Room Three, reaching back to feel my bare neck about fifty times along the way.

How could I be so stupid? Why did I let the paper pull me to it? Why didn't I look back over my shoulder first? Why didn't I just follow Misha instead?

Excited chatter ceases as I enter the classroom and all the girls drop their eyes, except the ones in my level. Eugenia's eyes bore into my forehead.

I hand Brother Michael his copy of the report and find my desk. I sit down and shield my eyes with my hand.

Thankfully, Sister Margaret continues with her lesson on "Multiple Harvests from a Single Renewable Crop." Her first example is the sunflower and its use for food, oil, feed, paper fiber, insulation, and compost, but she moves onto other examples, too: trees, soybeans, clover, oats, canola, garlic, and flax. Later, Brother Michael teaches how poisons and their antidotes are often found in the same ecosystem. I just tell myself to take notes, not to worry about Serenity or Mom, not to think about the Library or Sister Millie's advice, just to hold myself together.

After school, I wait on the edge of the schoolyard for my brother. Some kids point at me and whisper. Then I remember that Scott stayed home today because of his ear.

I hurry towards home, only because there is nowhere else to go. The sun feels hot on my neck and I kick at stones, frustrated. When I open the farmhouse door, Scott runs to greet me and hugs my waist. I pat his back, and then pry him off, putting the note from Sister Millie onto the kitchen table.

I pour a glass of water from the pitcher on the table and gulp it down.

"What happened to your hair?" he yells as Mom shuffles into the room.

She screams when she sees me and hollers for my dad in the barn. I'm sent to my room. No supper. No Remote. No lecture.

I sit against my bed on the floor, wondering when they'll come upstairs, wondering what they'll say, wondering how much worse things will get.

I pull out my purple book and stare at a blank page, my mind all jumbled, thinking about a hundred things, but then finding a big, black space where a thought should be. Finally, I think I hear feet on the steps, so I hide my book, just before the door opens.

Dad looks unsure, Mom disappointed, her face wrinkled. I never thought of her as old before, but she seems suddenly to have aged. She should be in bed.

I bite my lip. I wish they'd just yell and scream. I hate the quiet, the silence.

"I guess you know what happened today. I can see your tear streaks, though you are trying to pretend that you are unperturbed," Mom says.

Dad takes a step closer. "You didn't just lose your hair today. You lost the respect of your peers, Father, the Brothers and Sisters … and the whole Community will always remember."

"I do understand, Dad," I say, bursting into new tears, though he doesn't even know yet what else was lost: Serenity, Eric, and my chosen Life Role.

"You've got so much work ahead of you, now," he says, his voice a little softer. "You've got to gain back all their trust and admiration and make Father and your teachers think they've made a mistake about you, let them know what you're capable of before the end of Harvest Break next month. I know that will come up fast, but a lot can happen between now and the end of October," he says, as his voice trails away.

"You could prove it to them that you didn't read the letter," Mom suggests.

"Father knows I did."

"Foolish girl!" Mom says, and then takes a big breath. "For months now, we've been watching you, and we've seen your attitude towards authority change. We used to think it was hormones, typical puberty stuff, or maybe that you were secretly planning an early marriage. Your dad and I decided months ago to let you work through these things on your own because you've always been such a good daughter and a bright student. You've always grasped things more quickly than your peers. But now we see that we didn't monitor you closely enough. We made too many concessions when you were younger. We taught you to read before your time, and then let you devour the discarded books from Millie. They were being pulped for good reasons, which we—I—ignored. Then we brought color into this home instead of being responsible role models to show you how to respect the entire Manifesto. We realize that we've failed as parents, but we *will* correct that immediately. You have no privileges now. Things will change, Katherine," Mom says, sniffing away angry tears and reaching for the doorknob, her hand shaking. To Dad she says, "Maybe we should burn the color."

"Go to bed," Dad says, following her. "You're upset."

As they leave, I hear Dad say, "I'll make dinner for you and Scott before my meeting. It'll be a late one." He closes my door.

Dad has a meeting?

Later I hear Mom shout from the hall. "We had a deal. We made the choice, and now this?" I don't know if she is yelling at Dad or just up to the rafters.

I think about their words as I lie on my bed, staring at the ceiling. I hear their voices downstairs, more arguing, and then much later, Trotter's neigh.

Why can't I just behave? Things could be good again. I wish I'd never read that letter. What did it all mean, anyway?

It must've been very important to get me into such trouble. I think back to what I read in the letter; so many words I don't know. I pick up my purple book and write what I remember.

August 11, 2021 - The words that changed my life:

Canada? - A former country; a breed of goose
Armed Forces - Army?
Legislation - Formal law in government?
Father is making more rules?
Funded - To do with money?
Office - Father's office?
Monthly report - Is this from the Community Leaders?
Departments - Parts of the Community?
Ruth - Who is she?

There are several things that bother me about this letter. Firstly, the word *funded* makes me think of money. Money was an enormous problem before the Ecological Revolution, and things evolved so that there was no middle class, just the wealthy and the starving. Sharing equitably without possessions in a Community is the only way for everyone to live fairly and live well.

Secondly, why would Ruth—Sister Ruth, I assume, though I don't know of anyone in the Community with this name—why would she write such a fancy letter—with color!—to Father? Why wouldn't she just talk to Father in person? And the other words in the letter—*legislation, departments,* and *Canada*—these are words that were used in government before the Ecological Revolution.

What does all this have to do with Father, with the Community, with me? There's so much mystery that seems important, so much I don't understand that seems essential. I wish I could recheck the wording of the letter.

There's only one place to do that. The idea presses in like an unwelcome guest. Steal into Father's office. Maybe the letter is still in his bag. Maybe there is information about Mom's appointment yesterday on Father's desk.

I'm so upset by the day that I actually consider this. Things can't get worse at home or school.

The thing is, I don't have much of a future here now. If I don't check out the contradictions I see, I'm always going to have these two voices; I'm always going to wonder. I'll get assigned manual labor next month, and Father and my parents will be disappointed. What have I got to lose? Eric. How would checking out Father's office affect him?

If I stuff my bed, my parents will never know I am gone. I can be back long before dawn. But what if I get caught? Is this risk worth it?

I think of Mom's appointment with Father, of her crying in the wagon. In my mind, I see Serenity, holding out her little hands for me to pick her up. "Carry me, Katherine," she begs. It all comes down to one thing. How badly do I want answers?

Noisy river rippling by
Boat and hook are in together
Both held by a line.

Four of us are all at play
Fishing, sailing, sleeping, writing
Far from work and time.
Dad pulls back, his rod dips down
Pulling, leaning, reeling, screaming
Calls to crowd around.

Scott runs first and drops his line
Boat glides swiftly, swirling quickly
Then stopped by a rock.

Boat seems lost and hands fly up
Tears flow softly, gently, sadly
Scott runs down the shore.

Leaving his rod, Dad shivers in
Wading, slipping, sloshing, sopping
Big fish swims away.

6
Wednesday Night, August 11, 2021

An hour after Scott has gone to bed, I've made my decision and then changed my mind about five more times. My heart feels like it has an irregular beat up near my ears and I decide to go one step at a time and turn back any time my task becomes impossible.

I stuff my bed to make it look as if I'm still there and then listen at my parents' door. Nothing. I carry only a candle with a holder and five wooden matches tucked into the pockets of my brown jacket. I creep across the kitchen and wait a few more minutes.

I hear crickets outside and the hoots of burrowing owls, but not a creak or twitch from upstairs. What if Dad comes back while I'm gone and checks to see if I'm asleep? Would he be fooled by the stuffed figure in my bed?

I take what feels like almost five minutes just to open and close the squeak-prone screen door. The cool night air refreshes me as I step off the porch, but then my chest tightens and my hands sweat and I feel like I can't breathe. I can't do this. This is crazy and irrational. It's night and I've *never* left the farm past twilight. It's wrong to do so now.

I try to go back inside, but my feet will not listen to my brain. I tell myself to just stand, to go to the outhouse. My bladder joins in then, and my feet consent to obey. Just to the outhouse and back to the porch, I tell myself. As I walk, I breathe deeply, in a meditative way, as Sister Millie suggested. But instead of letting go of my questions, I focus on them until I remember that Serenity is somewhere in the dark, too, scared and alone, and she needs me to find her. And I resolve to try, or at least to join her in the dark under the same sky. Stealing in the shadows, I sneak along the dirt road from our farmhouse and continue past the school, Library, and Residential Areas. The stars and half-moon are the only lights I see, but my eyes adjust quickly.

With every step, I'm prepared to dart into the sunflowers at the sides of the lane if I hear Trotter's hooves. But as the minutes pass, I start to worry. Did Dad go home another way? Where was his meeting? And what kind of group meets after dark?

My legs are twitchy by the time I approach the Town Circle. The streets are dark and I move in the shadows past the rows of identical two-leveled wooden buildings. With drapes covering every window, it is difficult to determine who in the town is still awake, though it must be well after midnight.

I approach the Main Community Building, the only stone and brick structure in the Town Circle. It is grand in scale, with three levels, including a basement, and steps leading to an arched entrance.

I climb the stairs but on my way up, I hear voices. I race back down to the street and hide behind a planter, right beside the building's steps. I am shaking like a wet cat after a dunking. My sloppy mistake almost led to being discovered. I breathe in deeply again; I tell myself over and over that I'm safe, that I could turn back anytime and no one would ever know. Serenity and Mom are worth risking this much for, and more.

Is more than one meeting taking place tonight? Then, is Dad's meeting at some farm? Do the farmers meet to discuss logistics of harvests? That makes sense.

Why did I decide to do this? I think of Mom and try to justify my disobedience. I can't do it right now. The voices descend the steps and seem to stop. I make myself as small as possible. As I squat and listen, I realize that I am sweating.

"But why would some people use their rations to brew alcohol?" a man asks. "Why invent new things, new color, when it serves no nutritional or functional purpose?"

"This is a by-product of surplus; the rations are too large." I recognize that voice: Sister Margaret, but instead of a singsong chime, her voice is clipped. "History shows us that when a society has more than its basic needs, the focus changes from community to an individual-based, free market economy."

"Perhaps we should encourage population growth," another female voice says.

"But then we'd have famine if there was flooding or cereal rot," Sister Margaret reminds her. "Babies aren't always the answer."

"Well, they're never the problem," the woman retorts.

Have I discovered a secret meeting of the Community Leaders? Is Sister Margaret one of the Community Leaders?

A chill shivers my spine. Could disobedience at school mean trouble with a Community Leader? No wonder Father knows everything. The Community Leaders report to him what happens all around them.

The voices fade as the people walk away. I collapse against the stone wall behind me. My legs cramp from squatting so long.

A Community Leaders' meeting must have just ended. In Dictation today, I learned that Father chooses anonymous Leaders for a lifetime of service. They cannot resign.

I decide to wait until I know that the building is empty. For a while, the only sound I hear is my own heavy breathing and beating heart. A few minutes later, more feet shuffle out of the building and down the steps. Though the voices sound familiar, I cannot distinguish between them in this larger group.

"We should find out who is stirring up grumblers about a gathering place," says a man with a deep voice.

I peek for white hair, possibly illuminated by moonlight.

"Imagine gathering after the work day for music, camaraderie. It would lead to revolutionary talk," another man says.

"Or affairs," a third man adds, and another gasps.

"I say we focus on sports," a nasal-voiced man says. "Teach the young ones coordination skills through competition. It will sap some of that energy."

Father is not in this group.

"New Leader of Agriculture—"

Who?

I strain for any kind of clue but can't glean anything else. It would be madness to enter the building without proof that Father has left. I resolve to wait, though my teeth chatter and I've become thirsty. A mangy, gray dog comes for a sniff and I shoo him away. He returns and I shake my arms and legs, trying to scare him. He crosses the square but returns several minutes later, this time more determined, more intense about what's in my pocket. I reach in, and feel a stale crust of bread, hard as a rock, something only the dog knew was there. I throw this onto the cobblestones, as far as I can send it. The dog runs to retrieve it, gulps it down, and then returns for more.

What if other leaders come out? I have to get the dog away.

I shake my arms and legs again, this time with more urgency. My foot makes contact, and the dog yelps and bolts away, his tail down.

More time passes and the sweat on my head and chest starts to feel cold. My empty stomach rumbles. Self-doubts revisit me. I try more deep breathing.

My tired body shifts for the hundredth time to find a comfortable position, and my thoughts linger on everything that happened today, but mostly on Serenity.

I rest my head on my knees, closing my eyes to better listen, but even as I do this, my eyes open to the sound of more footsteps. My pulse races.

I crouch to see who is on the steps. There's Father's silver hair and ... Dad?

This was his meeting? Dad—a Community Leader? All my strength seeps away and I curl into a ball against the planter, fully aware that, if discovered, I will have no excuse. Would Dad protect me? He loves me, right? Overhanging plants cover my head and I carefully breathe in and out.

"So, as you can see from the media I've shown you, there is no other way. Soon you will believe as strongly as the others do, but for now, you must trust me." Father almost whispers, but I can still hear him.

Believe what?

"I have to think … this is overwhelming," Dad says, his voice wavering with emotion. He begins to walk away.

What's so overwhelming for Dad? What is *media* and how did Father show it to Dad? When did he join the Community Leaders? And why would he get asked to join when he failed as a youth and was assigned manual labor as his Life Role?

"I've known you all your life, ever since you were a scrappy newborn. Haven't I always advocated for your best interests?" Father pleads, calling after Dad. "Wasn't I the one who paired you with Mary?"

I dare to look now, out through the plants, my breath shallow.

Dad's footsteps stop and he comes back to Father, hands in fists, jaw clenched.

"You know, that was a stroke of genius, crafting the Manifesto after the Aunts and Uncles disappeared—or did they? We were young and naïve, hormonal, shocked … grieved at the implications of suddenly being left alone, of realizing that our guardians were beyond our reach, past the trees and grasslands, their bodies dead and rotting, picked apart by carrion, maggot-loving birds! And you, always pushing the Manifesto, promising that it would ensure our survival. How can I trust you, when your hand has been heavy on me my whole life? How can I believe you, when I realize I am no longer free?" Dad's voice breaks here, and I hear him sniff, see him wipe his face. Is he crying?

I've never heard him talk this way before. Even when my parents argue, Mom is the one with the shrill voice; Dad is the one to nod and swallow his replies—though his face always gives me the impression they taste like vinegar.

"You are freer than they are," Father implores, pointing back towards his office.

"We made a deal, Mary and I, and it didn't include this," Dad says, more to himself as he stumbles away.

"Don't tell her!" Father calls after him. "You'd be a fool. You'd hurt her."

What does Dad know that would cause my mom pain?

For what feels too long, I silently beg Father to leave, but his shoes seem rooted where they are planted. Finally, I hear Father's deep sigh, and he lumbers away, back beyond the steps.

My body relaxes and I shift to watch him walk home. Father strides down past about ten of the houses, opens a door and goes inside. Relief fills my shaking limbs. I feel weak, drained, and although I cannot articulate why, defeated.

Trotter's hooves startle me then and I withdraw into the shadows again. He whinnies as he passes by—does he catch my scent?—but Dad's pace doesn't falter and the rhythmic clippity-clops diminish until all that is left, shaking in the silence, is me.

Dad knows more than me so I can trust him, right? I can quiet my questions and let him make the right choices for our family. But Dad might not know what I do, and for this reason, I decide to wait.

I don't know if others will come out and if Father will return. I think about Serenity and imagine a crazy possibility. If she is in this building, I could take her home tonight. I imagine Anna's face when she sees Serenity again.

Then I turn my thoughts back to the paper in Father's bag.

The moon moves. It's as safe as it's going to be.

My creaky body stands and enjoys the luxury of a stretch but even as I do this, I dare not move my eyes from the direction of Father's home.

Like a barn owl, I swoop silently up the stairs and open, with both hands, the heavy wooden door of the Main Community Building. The deep black hall frightens me and I rest against the wall. Is someone still here?

When I can hear again, when my heart's pounding has quieted, I feel my way down the hall to Father's office. My fingers recognize the carved sign on Father's door; I turn the knob but nothing happens. The door is broken, stuck, and immovable. My hands shake impossibly as I try several times to light the candle in my pocket. I smother the matchstick between my fingers—comfort the burn with my spit, then put the evidence into my pocket. I must leave behind no clues.

The dim glow illuminates the hall and I study the door. Has it been nailed shut? Why would a door not work?

The door doesn't look broken. I slide to the floor and blow out the candle. Now what? Are all the doors in the building broken, too?

I get up then, and put the candle back in my pocket. I tiptoe down the hall and try every door. One door leads downstairs to the empty, windowless assembly room in the basement. I spare a second match to light the candle again and look around. Chairs in stacks of ten or so line the brick walls, but no other rooms lead off this space. I take the stairs then to the top floor, and a trip around reveals many undesignated, sparsely furnished rooms, but no Serenity. I was hoping she would be here but, of course, it's just my leaping mind at work again.

Wax from my candle drips down onto the fist clenching it, but I barely notice, even though it burns hot. I tolerate this pain rather than have wax drip around the halls and betray the presence of an intruder tomorrow.

The main floor space includes a large room with dining tables, a kitchen, and Father's office. A door from the kitchen is also broken, and could possibly lead to Father's examination room, if it worked. It seems coincidental that two doors are stuck, and I realize then they are not broken; they are fixed shut on purpose.

My brain begins to work faster then. If they are fixed shut on purpose, it is because there is something inside that is worth protecting. There must be something in the office, something that can't be shared, like the letter. Maybe there is information about Mom's tears or a clue about where Serenity has gone.

I rattle the door in frustration but it still will not open.

How can I get inside to find out? If I damage the door to get in, Father will know someone was here. Then I have an idea; I blow out the candle and return it to my pocket.

I look out the kitchen window, the one near Father's door. I open it and see a stone ledge outside, designed to support the second level brick walls. I crawl out the window—it's really only Dad's height to the ground—and balance on the ledge, holding onto the window sill with one hand while reaching with the other for Father's window. I press my palm to the pane then, but it barely budges, though I use my full strength. If I just had something to wedge into the tiny space I've created.

Back in the kitchen, I find a metal spoon that could work, and climb back out to pry Father's window open. The gap widens and I push it up. Success!

In Father's examination room, I discover that my candle's wick has broken off. I check that Father's drapes are still closed and then light his oil lantern. It's not difficult to do this in the dark as I have had many nights of practice alone in my room.

On Father's desk is a bizarre instrument, shaped like a thin, silver metal book. On one side is a smooth black rectangle, which bears some similarity to the Remote. Below and attached to it is a panel with uniform buttons of the alphabet, and all kinds of symbols that I do not recognize.

I touch the silver book, and discover that it is warm. Did Father read this thing to Dad?

There are many papers on Father's desk, but I move my attention to the wooden cabinet behind it. It vexes me for a few minutes because the doors are also stuck closed, secured by tiny, metal devices.

I try the drawers of Father's desk but they won't open, either. Why would Father prevent access to these Community cupboards? And where is the leather bag Father brought with him to the Library?

Looking around, I begin to despair. It is nowhere to be found. I'll just have to discover what I can from the papers on his desk. I tell myself to hurry, that I've been too long in this building and Father could still return, especially if he was unable to sleep after his upsetting conversation with Dad. If I have never heard Dad speak his mind like that, I'm sure Father hasn't, either.

The desk papers are organized into trays, and the rock weights have been moved to the edge of Father's desk. I turn over pages from the first tray, careful not to get them out of order, or crease the corners. Most of it appears to be a list of the Community members, close to four hundred names in all. The names are printed much smaller than the typewritten words in the Library's books.

Next to these names are a series of numbers and percentages under the heading *Retinal Scan Weekly Diagnostic Informational Scores*. What is a retinal scan and how is it performed weekly on the entire Community?

I study the scores of my family. There is a star next to my name and my scores are filled in with pencil. There are no markings next to Dad, but Mom's and Scott's names are circled. I wish I understood what this means.

I search out Anna's family's scores. There are machine-recorded scores next to the names of everyone in her large family, but Serenity's name is circled and crossed out. Three letters tell why: CHS.

I suck in my breath. Were her scores somehow connected with her disappearance and CHS, whatever that is? Was it a bad thing that her name was circled? Could Mom and Scott be in danger then, also? Does Dad know? What would he do if he knew? How well do I even know him?

I think about that, my eyes filling with tears. I don't know my Dad, might never really know him or how he thinks. I can never ask him what I need to know.

Trembling, I put the papers back in the first tray and reach for the ones in another.

This new tray is all facts, figures, and dates. They are also definitely not the product of a typewriter as some pages have fancy graphs—with color.

I find an interesting page half-way down the pile, titled *Shipping and Inventory Schedule*. I scan the dates and they fall evenly on the first and fifteenth of every month. I see that there is a shipment on the fifteenth, four days away. A shipment from where? To where?

My nerves tingle like when I have a fever. The top sheet of the last tray has the heading *Community Notes for Records: Data Entry.*

The pages are filled with handwritten notes and observations. I flip to the last page and start reading backwards to find anything familiar. At the top of the second to last page are the notes from my family's visit.

Scott: another ear infection or possible B21 virus, Ménière's Disease, or even Tinnitus. Possible impending hearing loss with referral needed.

Scott could lose his hearing? What is a referral? My vision swims a bit, and I am drawn back to the rest of the page's entry.

Katherine: normal retinal scans. Administered first warning.

I had a scan? Was Father's talk my first warning? I don't understand this. I feel like a Level One student in a Level Ten class. The only thing Father did besides ask me questions was shine the red light through my eyes.

The Retinal Scan Scores must be connected to the red light. Retinal must refer to some part of the eye. A horrifying thought occurs to me: the red light during Remote could be a retinal test. How else could the doctor get all these numbers and percentages each week? But then, how does the light record numbers?

My stomach lurches and I decide never to watch Remote again. I shuffle the papers back, and then remember about Mom.

Mary. Miscarriage. Genetic complications. Male.

I gasp! The last four words reverberate and echo in my brain. My Mom was pregnant. She lost another baby, a boy. Did Dad find this out tonight, too? Is that why he was mad at Father?

I start to cry for her, for me. I would have enjoyed another baby brother. A tear falls on Father's desk and I remember where I am. I blot the tear with my elbow and carefully pile the papers back together. I check the room to make sure all is as it should be, then I turn down the lamp, slip through the drapes, and climb out the window, closing it on the other side. I remember my palm print on Father's window, and slide out of my jacket so I can rub the glass clean with it. As I do, the candle falls, and the spoon too, clattering on the cobblestones below.

I freeze, realizing I might have just moments before I am discovered. I yank the kitchen window closed behind me and jump to the darkness below.

Nausea like I've never known swirls up near my vocal cords. On the cobblestones, I reach with both hands for the metal spoon—and find it—but the candle has rolled somewhere out of my reach.

Not daring to stay any longer, I edge my way in the shadows, back towards the front of the building. Then I am sick, heaving all my swirling stomach's putrid acid, into the planter.

> *I watched*
> *The sunset tonight.*
> *I timed it going down and found*
> *As I ducked my head down to write*
> *Every time I looked up*
> *It had moved.*
> *Amazing.*

7

Thursday, Early Morning, August 12, 2021

Dad says the darkest part of the night is right before dawn and that's the time I get back to the farmhouse. My eyes are puffy-sore from weeping and despite all the heavy thoughts in my brain, I long for a safe, warm bed and the respite I always find in sleep.

Safe upstairs in my room, I light the lantern and examine the bed. It's still stuffed as I left it. Was I missed tonight? I think of my clumsy mistake with the candle, of how close I came to being found out. I think also of the metal spoon I buried in a ditch along the way home.

These new secrets are jabbering nonstop in my head and there's just one way I know to let them go. But before I write down my secret thoughts, there's something I need to do first.

I change out of my dirty clothes, climb into bed, and retrieve my book bag and purple notebook. Remembering the little piece of wood from the wagon, I rip slivers from the side until it fits in the bottom of my writing box. Then I measure and cut my purple book from three sides until it fits, careful to collect all the scraps and bits back into my bag. My beautiful purple book is shabby, like my hair, but neither can be helped tonight.

My empty, upset stomach churns and gurgles but I tell it to be quiet, as I would a barking dog. Some things are more important than food.

I pick up my pencil and write down what I've learned tonight and some of my questions, the loudest ones first. And as I do, it's like I'm in a room packed with people, crushed together so tight I can barely breathe. And each time I write down a sentence, one of these people leaves the room and I get back a bit more space to breathe.

What is CHS?

Was there something wrong with Serenity? What was that?

What can I do to protect Mom and Scott from disappearing like Serenity?

Why does it matter to Father if babies are born with genetic complications?

Will Scott lose his hearing? How would I know?

How does the red light get info about my health?

What is a referral?

When and why did Dad join the Community Leaders?

What is the shipment that takes place the first and fifteenth of every month?

How do these shipments affect the Community?

What goes out? What comes in?

What is media?

I think about Anna, worried about Father upstairs questioning her parents, and how she tried to comfort *him*. But Father's office notes are proof that what happened to Serenity had something to do with her health. If she was lost, or injured, or attacked, Father would not have circled her name, crossed it out, and written CHS. What happened to Serenity had something to do with the red light scores, something medical. Why didn't Father just tell what he learned to Anna and her parents? And why did he allow Serenity to be taken in the night?

I think about these questions and how to respond. First, I decide to double-check that the retinal scan is really linked with the red light. To do this, I get the dictionary from under my mattress, the one I saved from being pulped years ago.

My stomach rolls, and I tiptoe to the kitchen for a handful of dried saskatoon berries, which I eat to settle my tummy. On the way out of the pantry, I see a crust of bread, so I grab that, too.

Back under the covers again—door closed—I tear big bread bites with my teeth while flipping through the dictionary.

> **retina** *n.* 1) A delicate, multi-layer, light sensitive membrane lining the inner eyeball and connected by the optic nerve to the brain.

I read this sentence three times. I don't understand how the Retinal Scan works but maybe the red light touches the retina and reads information from my brain. If there *is* something wrong with Mom or Scott, they shouldn't watch Remote or Father could monitor their health and make a decision about them. But if I'm grounded from Remote, as I am now, how can I stop them?

The word *media* is a dead end clue.

media *n.* 1) *pl.* of medium.
medium *adj.* 1) having a middle position; moderate.
Media *n.* 1) ancient country in former sw Asia

The entry for *referral* is more puzzling. There's no definition given, so I can only guess from the definition of *refer: send or direct for information, help, or action.*

Who would Father refer Scott to, for help, information, or action about his hearing? Who could possibly know more about how to help our bodies than Father?

I read about the word *shipment.*

shipment *n.* 1) The act of shipping
shipping *n.* 1) Ships collectively; also tonnage. 2) The act of shipping.

I close the dictionary. The root word of *shipping* is a word I know: *ship*. Before the revolution, trade occurred between communities all over the world with an exchange of cargo or goods; enormous boats, like the *Titanic*, moved much of it across seas. There are no oceans near our Community, only a river and a lake.

Could cargo be moved in through the river, cargo such as wires for the Remote and some of Father's gadgets? Could there be another Community near ours? Who are we shipping to, and who is shipping to us? Could other humans be alive beyond our forests and wild grass fields? Could the *sky scratchings*—the white lines that move high on the cloudless blue skies—be actual evidence of another community and not of atmospheric instability, as I've been told?

I imagine our river would be problematic for secretive work twice a month; it is a common place for Roles and recreation. You'd think, though, there'd be rumors of ships arriving at odd hours, especially during summer months before Harvest when Lake Travel is permitted … or during winter when sections of it freeze completely.

I open my dictionary again for the definition of *ship*.

> **ship** *n*. 1) Any vessel suitable for deep water navigation; also its personnel. 2) A seagoing vessel with three masts …

How could a boat like this travel up our river undetected? What if there was no wind?

> 3) An airship or airplane …

Could cargo be transported into the Community by air? Two days ago, I remember thinking that school wasn't relevant, but this is the subject Sister Margaret was teaching us about on Tuesday in Dictation for Fact Drill. Before the Ecological Revolution, people and cargo were transported across the planet by air as well as by ships. It's not possible now because of Earth's unstable atmosphere. The Aunts and Uncles didn't return from the search party because of pockets of deadly, unstable air existing outside the Community. Airplane engines need air.

But what if Father and the Leaders are wrong about the Aunts and Uncles? Perhaps they didn't die. And what if there isn't an unstable environment outside the Community? Then there might be other life on this planet. The Aunts and Uncles could still be out there. What if air transport is still possible?

My mind is racing. I'm thinking about the note in the cornfield.

> *Everything is not as it seems.*
> *I've seen the outside come*
> *Through the sky*

What other way is there *through the sky*? Air travel must be possible. It seems more likely than boats on a river. But then, if everything I've been taught is a lie, then the opposite of all things is plausible. Or is it? How can I tell truth from lies? And why would Father and the Community Leaders intentionally lie to everyone?

I think of Dad. Why would Dad become a Community Leader if they lie about the truth outside? Why would Dad want to ignore problems?

I have to find the landing area. Sister Margaret said that aircraft needed a large strip of ground with which to take off and land on. I must find that in four days. No! This is now the early morning of the twelfth, so I have three days. What do I do then? I could re-check the wording of the note in the cornfield, now that I have a safe place to hide it.

I close my purple book and place it under the wood at the bottom of my writing box. All my ink and other writing materials hide the false bottom.

If only my thoughts could diminish as easily as the flame in my oil lantern. Eventually, though, after more wrestling, I give over my greatest worry to the Planet Keeper. I pray that I may never fail my brother or wake to find him gone.

I dream that Serenity is calling me from the wheat field.

Scott is shaking me. "Wake up, Katherine. Wake up!"

I pull the blankets over my head. My heavy eyes feel red-sore and my stomach is queasy.

"We'll be late for school," he says, pulling at my arm.

I ignore him until he starts jumping on my bed.

"Please stop! I'm sick."

His footsteps scuttle down the hall. I startle awake to Dad checking my forehead with the back of his hand. Was I just asleep?

"She's sick," Scott tells him.

I try to get up. "Really, I'm okay." I move my stiff, groggy body to the edge of the bed, eyes still shut.

"You know the rules. No absence from school unless authorized by Father."

I open my eyes and squint up at Dad, swallowing hard.

Dad needs an excuse why I can't go to school, but I can't frame a sensible sentence. I resign myself to going. Maybe Sister Margaret or Brother Michael will send me home. I try to think: has that ever happened?

My brain starts to remember. My retinal scan was fine two days ago. Father will know I'm perfectly healthy. It would be suspicious to be away the day after my second warning. I feel the back of my neck. Father will know I'm away because of my punishment.

I have to get ready for school. I have to pretend that nothing has changed, that I don't know everyone's secrets—Father, Dad, Mom, Serenity.

Dad is still watching me. I guess he sees something pathetic because he surprises me.

"Stay in bed. With Scott's ear infection, it's just as well that you both stay home. We'll deal with teachers tomorrow."

I lie back, relieved.

"At noon, fix lunch. Your mom needs to rest. You'll still have to do your afternoon chores and hers, too. Scott can help me around the farm this morning, but I'll need to help hay this afternoon."

Mom. I sit up again. I know why she's in bed and it's horrible. I need to go to school. I have to find out about the shipment, the landing area, Anna …

Dad looks at me, puzzled. "Peace," he tells me, gently pushing my shoulder back to the mattress.

Too tired to fight, I submit. Besides, my teachers will notice a change in me today. I'll score lower on my Fact Drills. And could I run in this heat to the Dairy? Or help in the Cannery? I'm already dizzy; I should stay home. What use am I going to be today, with two hours sleep?

"I'll fix lunch," I mumble.

Dad puffs out his cheeks and exhales slowly, his brow wrinkled in thought. Is he still mad? Is he thinking about his meeting? Why is he looking at me like that? Is that a tear in his eye? He doesn't let me know and, once again, just leaves the room with the entirety of his thoughts.

I think of Mom. My heart feels heavy and I can hardly explain why. It has something to do with her rye bread and low table and all the things she does for me and Scott, the way she held back her sobs until we were out of the Town Circle; something to do with how difficult I can be. All along, I've thought I was the intelligent one, the one who sees the problems. I assumed that I'm the only one willing to risk for the truth. I've judged Mom because I thought she was a simpleton to believe in a perfect Community. Now I believe that Mom knows things she doesn't talk about and I feel differently about her, loyal, protective, admiring.

Her grief has touched me. Maybe I don't understand her, but there is something very brave about her wanting to love, wanting to grow life in an imperfect place.

> *My words spill onto the page*
> *Like water from a bucket*
> *Water from the laundry bucket*
> *I bring from the well,*
> *Soapy bubbles everywhere.*

8

Thursday, August 12, 2021

Scott is watching me. I blanket my head and groan.

"Mom says it's time to make lunch."

My feet are sore. That's the first thing I notice when I bring them to the floor.

"What happened to your hair?" Scott asks, his voice soft.

Rubbing my eyes, I remember his name circled—and then imagine it crossed out. I reach for him and hold him tight. "I could never lose you," I whisper.

Scott wiggles away. "Let's play hide and seek."

"It will have to be later," I tell him, walking past Mom's room.

"Come here, Katherine." Mom is in her rocking chair, darning socks by the window. Putting her sewing down, she folds her arms and leans back into the chair.

"Use a jar of chicken stock to make a soup. Add lots of vegetables. You know, just the way your dad likes it."

I nod and begin to back away. She means the recipe from my Home Skills class. It's my favorite thing to cook, but today it seems like a lot of work.

My eyes tear a bit when I remember last night and I blink to avoid crying. As an afterthought, I offer tea. She nods, but then glances away again, out the window.

Downstairs, I reach for a pitcher to fill the kettle. My bladder screams for relief at the rushing sound of water. I slip into my clogs by the kitchen door and dash to the outhouse just in time.

I wash my hands in the kitchen basin and check inside the stove. Glowing embers remain from breakfast and I stir them up and add another chunk of wood. Then I fill the pitcher again with more water from our pump house. While I'm doing this, my hand hurts and I look down and see blistered red skin near my left thumb. Confused for a minute, I examine it and then remember the dripping wax from last night. What kind of salve might Mom have that would help this heal?

I'm still thinking of this while I walk to the kitchen with the pitcher. The house is quiet—where's Scott? I put the kettle on and go to find him.

Puzzles and wood figures are strewn on the floor. Evidently, he has exhausted playing with every toy Dad has made for him. Scott is in his hiding spot, under the bed.

"Come out," I say. "I need your help with the soup. We have to do our chores."

Scott moves away and folds his arms across his chest. He's been crying.

"You're upset."

"You don't want to be my friend anymore," he blurts out.

I'm too tired for this! But I fight the urge and, instead, reach for his hand. "That's not true."

"You won't talk to me."

"Oh, Scott," I say gently. He doesn't understand.

"What?"

Didn't he hear me?

"It was an awful day yesterday," I say a little louder, remembering that his ear is still plugged up with wool. It's just an infection; he's not losing his hearing, right?

"We always used to talk," Scott reminds me, his lip quivering.

"We still can."

"No, we can't. You've been different since the wagon." At this, he bursts into new tears.

I pull my brother from under the bed and take him into my arms. He resists me at first but as I hold on, he softens, sobbing again.

"Scott, in the wagon, I said we can't talk using questions."

"You mumble so much. I can't hear you."

"I said we couldn't talk using questions," I say, louder.

"Then we can't talk at all!"

"Of course we can."

"I just tried."

"We are *now*." I look at my brother and am surprised by what I see behind those chubby fingers, rubbing away the tears. Scott doesn't look sad or angry—he looks afraid, as if he is lost.

Is he afraid of losing me, too? Because I tell him we have to change the way we are together and then he sees me in trouble, but doesn't understand why? He doesn't know why Mom and Dad are mad, or how I got in trouble at school. Why is it so hard to pursue truth and be mindful of his feelings at the same time? I'm not his Mom. Why do I sometimes feel like it?

"It's going to be okay," I tell Scott, holding him tight again.

He's quiet a minute, then says, "Did they really cut your hair at school because you asked too many questions?"

"Ask me what you want but in a different way," I tell him, moving so that we're seated side by side. I stretch my neck to soothe a muscle spasm in my shoulder.

"What?"

"Ask me what you want without a question," I say, a bit louder.

"I can't."

"Try." My hand is still sore. Which salve: comfrey, yarrow, or both?

"Did you lose your hair because you asked questions?"

I fight the urge to give up, to let Scott deal with his emotions on his own. He's trying so hard. I swallow my frustration and answer his question.

"My teachers cut my hair because I didn't reverence Father yesterday. It was embarrassing and I still feel upset about it."

Scott uncrosses his arms. I realize I am sitting on something, a wooden bird figure; I shift to a more comfortable position.

I continue. "My teachers might not have reacted so harshly if I'd been a more respectful student all along. Scott, you need to learn that questions are another way of not showing respect."

Scott's eyes are wide, his mouth open. "Will they shave my head if I keep asking questions?"

Are questions just natural to a child? "They won't tolerate it when you're older, so you might as well learn now."

"But I don't know how," he says, flopping his arms down to the floor.

"That's okay, Scott. No one expects you to change right away. I'm older than you. For now, just try to listen better."

Scott looks down at some of his wooden farm animals as I stand up. I look at my blister and try to navigate a safe path out of his room.

"You have really got to clean this room up. It's a pig sty."

"Can't you help me?"

"No, I have got to make the soup and … the *tea*!" I hurry downstairs to the kitchen to find it all steamy with the kettle boiled dry. I grab the oven mitts to refill it. My sore hand feels scalded just being near the steamy heat.

I chip off a piece of ice, put it onto my blister, and then wrap my hand in a strip of rag. Looking down, I notice that I'm still in my nightclothes. In my room upstairs, I examine the Community uniform I wore yesterday but find that it is filthy from sitting on the cobblestones behind the planter. I should wash this today so Mom doesn't find it tomorrow while I'm at school and connect the state of these clothes with my injured hand.

The ice drips wet but the burn feels numbed. I dress in a clean uniform and pick up my hairbrush. It's so strange not to have to brush past my shoulders; strange not to need a few minutes just to smooth out the tangles and knots. In my looking glass, I examine my face for signs of beauty, but conclude that I look as if I've been in a fight. My face is pale; my eyes are puffy and bloodshot; my hair is lopsided and ugly. Will Eric care? I push all these thoughts from my mind and go make the tea.

While it steeps, I get an assortment of vegetables from the pantry and garden: carrots, beets, potatoes, green beans, onion, and some herbs, too. I also reach for the jar of chicken stock I labeled. Mom and I boiled it from a chicken Dad butchered two weeks ago.

Then I take the tea to Mom, now asleep in her chair, too tired to wait for it. I leave it on the little table beside her and hope she has a good rest.

I need to hurry so lunch will be ready when Mom awakes. Peeling the vegetables, I place them in the soup pot with the boiling broth. I top it up with kettle water, add some of the leftover mashed potatoes, and season with dried Summer Savory. It's not anything fancy but it will taste good to Dad, who has been out in the field all morning. He never complains about my cooking.

I find the comfrey salve in the pantry then, rub it on my burn, and hang the rag bandage to dry. In the pump house, I pre-soak my filthy uniform—and other soiled clothing I find in the house, further hiding any evidence of last night.

I set the table and check on Scott. He's put away half his toys but he's lying on the floor, flying a pig around in the air. This strikes me as ridiculous and I start to laugh.

"Scott, pigs don't fly."

He laughs, too. "This one does."

"But the air outside the Community is unstable," I recite, tongue in cheek.

Scott doesn't miss a beat. "It's flying inside our Community."

Still smiling, I help my brother clean up the rest of his room and pair his socks. I pick up a book and tell him to come read with me.

We step downstairs as Dad comes in from outside. His face looks dark as the clouds of a summer squall, and his eyes seem ready for a downpour. Is Dad going to cry? Scott misses this and runs for a hug.

I bite my lip and check the soup. Is Dad thinking about his secret talk with Father?

"I hope your ear feels better," Dad says.

"It's all plugged," Scott replies.

Dad ignores Scott's answer and rubs his hands together. "So hungry."

"A few more minutes," I say, putting down the stirring spoon, then turning away to look out the window at the pump house. "Sorry."

Dad picks up the kitchen scraps bucket. "Let's go feed the pigs, Scott. There was a weasel in the barn last night. You won't believe the mess one of those little monsters can make, and they're impossible to catch. I need to have Brother Jack, the Trapper, take a look."

Scott runs for his slip-on clogs and races Dad out the door.

I rest against the sill, my head in my hands. Inside, I want to collapse, but my thoughts turn, instead, to last night.

Should I worry about the problems I see if Dad is a Community Leader? How much does Dad know? Does he know about Mom's appointment, the syringe, and *genetic complications*? Does he know that if Scott's hearing doesn't improve, he could be referred—whatever that is? And does he know what happens when someone's name is circled and crossed out?

Maybe Dad and I know different secrets. Maybe he has been broken by manual labor and by what he learned last night. But why, if Dad was such a difficult student at school, is he being invited to join the Community Leaders? And why now?

What does Mom know? What was the syringe for? What deal did Mom make with Dad?

Can I outgrow my questions and live down my second warning? Would I want to? Should I try?

I think the soup tastes bland so I put salt and dried herbs on the table, but no one adds these to their bowls except me. When we're all done, I get a start on the dishes, pouring the still hot water from the kettle into our washbasin, and then adding a pinch of lard soap shavings. My burn screams to me as I do this and I bite my lip. Dad leans back in his chair—Scott in his lap—and looks at Mom, drawing her to him with his eyes.

"I hope you're feeling stronger," he says, his voice husky, maybe even apologetic.

"I slept in the rocker most of the morning," Mom replies, wincing a bit. "Scott, come over here."

My brother kneels on the floor, his head in her lap, as she uncorks the wool from his ear.

"I'll need the medicine from Father," Mom says in my direction. Her voice is curt; I'll get no compliments today for anything I do. I'm sure she'll be mad about my hair until it grows to the middle of my back. I find new wool and the glass vial and hand them to her.

"Cold," Scott whines, as Mom squeezes new drops into his ear.

"This is helping," Mom says, and strokes the blond, sweaty-boy hair behind his ear, lingering to trace her fingertips along the outer ridges. Scott melts into her lap like butter.

"Tomorrow, you will both go back to school," Dad tells us.

I nod and wipe the kitchen table; Scott doesn't move and looks about ready to fall asleep, his eyes closed.

"Brian," Mom says, "I'd like to fix Katherine's hair—it's so uneven. But I can leave it if you think it best."

Dad puffs his cheeks full of air and then exhales slowly. I catch my breath and listen for his answer while walking back to the washbasin.

"I don't care," he says. I turn and see him blinking, as if he has something in his eyes.

Mom looks at me, then chides my father. "Of course it matters. I think losing her hair is one thing and presenting an ugly spectacle is another. She'll still have hair like a boy's, but at least it won't look like it was cut with pruning shears."

"I wouldn't trim Trotter's mane with that little care," Dad agrees, in an effort to appease her, "even if he were a pain in the backside."

"But Millie cares," Mom tells him. "She was just following orders and administered what Katherine deserved."

"Right," Dad says, though I'm quite sure he means the opposite.

Picking up the dish towel, I start to dry our bowls, pretending to ignore my parents.

Mom lowers her voice. "There's no chance of her getting married this year with hair like that. I can be relieved there, at least."

Dad kisses her then, cupping her chin in his coarse hand, lingering a few extra seconds before wordlessly leaving again for what I expect is the hay fields.

Mom taps Scott on the shoulder. "Outdoor play time," she tells him. "Go water and weed your little garden."

"What?" he asks.

Mom adjusts his wool again and pats him on the back. "Out to play, honey," she says, a little louder than before, opening the screen door for him, and a few windows, too. "It's hot in here."

I look at the stove. "Just embers now."

Mom rummages for the hairbrush and scissors while I wipe all the counters and cover any food that might attract flies or insects with fine wire colanders. I leave the pot of leftover soup on the stove to cool, knowing that if I put it in the icebox now, the heat will accelerate the melting of our ice ration. Mom waits for me to finish fussing with the cleaning.

"Go get a towel," she tells me, looking out the window at Scott, who is picking up kindling that Dad is chopping from log chunks. Then Dad goes into the barn with his ax and comes out with Trotter's saddle. How long will he have to hay this afternoon?

Mom starts to brush my hair. When I was younger, I loved this; I'd feel all tingly from my neck all the way down my spine, as if every follicle on the skin of my body was awake. But today's strokes are impatient, choppy, and rough.

"Honestly! It's going to take an hour to fix this." Mom pours water from the pitcher onto my head, which shocks me into a shudder and soaks my shoulders. I don't even gasp—it's that refreshing.

She straightens my head firmly. I hear her breath at the back of my head as she studies where to begin.

I hate the silence. My mind searches for a safe topic.

"I wonder about life when you were younger," I say, finally.

"Hmm."

"To be raised by the Uncles and Aunts, instead of parents," I probe. Who pushed my mom out of her womb? Who labored and cried as she was born? Who cut my mom's umbilical cord? What was that woman—my grandmother—like?

"Oh," she says, her voice trailing off, "to never know your parents; to always wonder who they were and how they died in the Ecological Revolution … these are questions for which I have never found peace."

"You question," I say.

Mom catches it, too, and she adds, "If it wasn't for Father and the Aunts and Uncles who saved us all as babies, you wouldn't be here. There would just be nothingness, an empty planet."

The scissors start then, and her fingers systematically pull at clumps of hair to trim.

She continues. "In the chaos of the Revolution, there was mass destruction and death—so much unstable fallout from the atomic bombs. A group of displaced people—fifty of them—clustered together, searching for resources and a habitable area, a place where they all could work together and survive. Along the way, they found us—one hundred abandoned infants left to die, our pasts unknown."

I know this part. "They gathered you and whatever else they found, and they stuffed the vehicles with what they'd need later— seeds, animals, tools, clothes, technology items—anything that might be helpful."

"Right. I don't know how long they looked, but, eventually, they found this region: a place with clean air and water untouched by radiation, as far as they could tell."

"Brother Michael said that the soil here ranges from sandy, to raw peat, to heavy clay, and that every kind of crop can grow here, from cereal to oil seed."

"That's right," Mom says, as the scissors continue.

"Lucky," I add. Coincidental?

"The Uncles and Aunts were very skilled," Mom says, with a sniff, "and they knew how to build a settlement. They raised us babies into adulthood."

"You called them Uncles and Aunts," I say, repeating her, willing her to keep talking. Do I push too hard? This is the most she has ever told me about this.

"They were very clear about not being our parents. They had lost so much in the Revolution that nothing else mattered to them anymore, except ensuring our survival and, in doing so, the survival of all humankind. We were *the last remaining hope* and they seemed to focus on us as their mission in life."

How could they know with any certainty that they were the only surviving community in the world? How do my parents deal with all these unanswered questions about the past?

"One hundred babies, fifty Uncles and Aunts, one Father," I say. Too perfectly proportioned?

"One Father," Mom says. "Father always seemed different to me … somehow … more personable. As the only adult trained in medicine, he knew everyone, of course, and was kept so busy. But even when we were all in the Big House—you'd know it as the warehouse—in our first domicile, with all the dorms and shared rooms, I remember him insisting he would read to us all, right before bed. It was very special and I looked forward to it each night.

"We'd huddle in, all hundred or so of us, up near the main central fireplace, and he'd tell the most fantastic stories, and act them out, even. I miss that, sometimes, and the noise, too. The farm can be so quiet at night. You'd think I'd have grown used to that by now." Her voice trails off, and her hands rest on my shoulders.

"So different," I say, after she picks up another clump of hair. Better?

"Our concepts of childhood and parenthood *are* different,"

Mom says. "But it doesn't matter. The Aunts and Uncles were right: the only goal is that the human species survives. That's the only thing that matters in the end, not how we're raised or what year we get our Life Roles. We just keep trying for life to continue," she says, and I hear her blow her nose with the kerchief from her pocket.

But what if civilization isn't just us? What if there are others out there trying to survive, too? Couldn't we help each other?

I think of living in the same building with Anna, Eric, and the Cowbirds. "Life all together would be wonderful … and awful," I say, finally. "Best friends and bullies together."

Mom is quiet for a minute. Have I said too much?

"You infer well," she says, finally. "Because you have some of both, I imagine. I didn't know that."

"A best friend makes life with bullies tolerable."

"Yes," Mom says. "I had Millie and your dad, but it doesn't serve to mention the others now. And you have Anna."

She waits for me to say more. Eric … a kiss and maybe a future? Eugenia and Prudence? But I can't open my mouth to say a word. And it feels hard to swallow, hard to say anything, because the mention of Anna has made me think again of someone else.

Does Mom know about Serenity? What would she say if I mentioned her?

"Serenity," I whisper, finally.

"What a sweetheart," Mom says, then thinks for a minute. "No, Rajesh and Rebekah weren't bullies to me; they are lovely, hardworking, generous people. Beks, Millie, and I shared a room with three others in the Big House for years."

Mom doesn't know about Serenity? If she did, wouldn't her voice betray it now? If Dad knows, he didn't tell Mom. Is this what Father told Dad to keep secret? Or maybe Mom doesn't know about Serenity because she hasn't seen anyone in town since her appointment, and Father hasn't mentioned Serenity on the Remote.

Mom keeps reminiscing. "As children, we stayed most of the day in a large common area. All the adults took care of all the kids, not just one or two in particular. We never felt lonely or felt we were alone; there were always people around, always someone to play with or talk to."

Mom stops and I turn around. She is looking out the window again.

"But you know how that ended," she says, then turns my head back around.

"Please tell," I say. "Please."

Mom waits a few minutes before answering. Have I been too direct? She sniffles. Is she crying? Will she stop talking now?

"I'll tell you, because you are about to become an adult, and because our lives together are about to change when you get your Life Role and move out or get married. I want you to tell your babies when they grow up so that this part of their story is never forgotten." Mom blows her nose into her kerchief, and then continues.

"We got our Life Roles, based on the skills we had been groomed for. By this time, the Community had a mill, a mine, a fishery, a cannery, a detached school building separate from the Big House, a library full of books, a Town Center, many storehouses, the residential area, farms with residences built ready-to-go—the Aunts and Uncles were always building and developing the entire area. Then Father paired us up and married everyone in the first Family Ceremony."

I nod then, and she holds my head still, to trim around my ears.

Did Mom love Dad then as she does now? What if some of the pairs didn't love each other but they still had to get married? A thought comes to me. Maybe my parents' marriage is rare. Maybe marriage for most people is just committing to a logical choice. I wish I could ask her. Could I still have a good life with Eric if I don't really know him?

"It was after the Ceremony that we were given separate residences, each one with a Remote, so we could still stay connected through Community news. It helped with the loneliness, the separation, and the quiet."

"And then I came along," I say.

"No. Many, many babies came along—not you, yet—your dad and I had to wait seven years for you. One day, Father gathered us for a meeting and informed everyone we needed more raw resources. We were a growing Community and it was time to explore more of the world, to find out what was outside."

Like *outside* through the sky?

"Dad volunteered to be a member of the party. I was pregnant with you then and I was afraid that Father would let him go, too. How I loved that Father refused him. Since we were the only pair that hadn't yet successfully birthed a child, Father said he needed Dad to stay, in case I went into early labor. He thought it was too much of a sacrifice for any other young family to spare a mom or dad for three weeks. The Aunts and Uncles decided then that only they would go. They had worked so hard to build the Community and they looked forward to a little rest, a little nomadic camping and adventure."

"They died … never returned," I say, under my breath. "Suffocated."

Mom stops cutting and steps back.

I turn and apologize. "Sorry. Brother Michael told us." Was I too blunt? After a minute, she brushes hair off my shoulders, and then cuts again at the base of my neck.

"It was summer, you know. That's why the Uncles and Aunts Memorial Garden is so important. Many of the plants and flowers have *powerful* memories for us. We remember collecting seed varieties in the early days and learning from the Uncles and Aunts how to propagate the plants you now see everywhere."

"Hmmm," I say. "I didn't ever think of that—plants holding memories."

Were the bodies of the Uncles and Aunts discovered and put into a mass grave? Where are they buried?

"They were excited to go." Mom sniffs again, then says, "After some debate about the details, it was decided that Father would remain to deliver any babies and Ruth would organize the details of the search. She thought if teams of five went off in ten directions, they could happily explore, and then return well before Harvest, when they would be essential again. They took supplies and provisions for three weeks, packed them all into back bags and waved good-bye."

Is that why we're told the air is unstable all around us? Must I believe that this Community exists as a circular pocket of life, surrounded by a circumference of death?

Mom is not cutting my hair now. We're in the room together, but in our own separate worlds of wonderings.

"Ruth ..." I say under my breath. But mom hears me and I catch my breath.

"Ruth." Mom sighs.

Was Ruth her favorite Aunt?

I turn in my chair to look at Mom; her eyes crinkle near the edges.

"If ever I had a Mom, it was Ruth. She had a way of looking right through my soul to find the right thing to say, before my mind had even formed the question. When I was a child and couldn't quite figure out how to lace my shoes or write my name—the other Aunts or Uncles could be so impatient—I'd go to Ruth and we'd find a quiet place and she'd teach me slowly, no pressure, no tears of frustration. When the babies wouldn't come and I despaired, Ruth let me shadow her on her nursing trips around the Community. She trusted me with the newborns while their moms recovered from birth. I learned how to wipe them down, check them over, wash them, diaper them—and then I'd swaddle them up tight with clean, newly spun wool and give them back to their moms. I loved Ruth, but then, so did everyone. She was involved in leadership and sometimes I wondered about her and Father ..." She looks at me then looks away. "I shouldn't talk in this manner—unfounded, silly talk."

"Don't worry," I say. "When I tell my babies, I'll forget that part." Father and Ruth? Was Father training Ruth as a doctor? Was it more than that?

A thought comes to me. Should I tell Mom about the letter? Would she want to know that Ruth didn't really die, that she's safe somewhere, writing colorful letters to Father?

"When Harvest came, and then later the snow, we feared the

worst. The tools and gear in their back bags were unsuitable for anything beyond summer camping. The Aunts and Uncles were resourceful, but unprepared to survive a severe winter without proper shelter. They would've come back if there was any way. I know this. Finally, we had to conclude that they all died. Father was heartbroken. Poor man! He still never alludes to any of this. I think he holds himself responsible, though I don't know why."

Mom's lip quivers and her eyes dew. I'm silent, hoping she doesn't cork up. Is this what it's like to have your Mom talk to you like an adult? Is Mom telling me all this now because she really sees our relationship as changing?

"I cried for months, thinking of Ruth suffocating alone somewhere, gasping for poison breath. What nightmares I had! And still, no adults could be spared to recover the bodies. We were resigned to grief and slow acceptance. There was nothing we could do to go back in time and stop the expedition, only survive, remember, and make sure no other risks like that were taken again."

"I'll tell my babies," I reassure Mom, giving her hand a squeeze. "I promise I won't forget."

She smiles, a sad smile, and then looks from my hair, to my shoulders, to our hands clasped together.

Mom's eyes stop here, and she picks up my hand to evaluate my burn.

"Your hand," she says, implying the need for an immediate explanation.

"Kettle burn," I lie.

"I have something for that," Mom tells me, walking off to the pantry. She passes me the comfrey salve. "Try this."

I unscrew the lid from the glass jar and slather more on the burn.

"Hmmm." Mom brushes the hair off my shoulders. "Done. Not perfect but better."

I feel along my head: the ends of my hair are straight now but significantly shorter.

"Thank you," I tell her, and check my looking glass. I'm a boy. I pinch my cheeks and lick my lips but it doesn't help; I just look like a flushed boy with tidy hair.

Returning downstairs, I see my mom in the porch swing, rocking slowly, a glass of water in her hand, her eyes somewhere off on the horizon.

I sweep up all the hair, and carry it out back behind the house. I stand there, eyes closed, looking up at the sky … and when I feel a breeze, I throw my hands in the air for the wind to carry this old part of me away.

That night in bed, I think more about my talk with Mom. Our conversation—though thick with details I always wondered about but was unable to ask—has made me realize something else. I now have two pieces of proof that there is life outside the Community. The note in the cornfield, and the letter from Ruth to Father; they both allude to something beyond here.

The issues are more defined for me now. It's not just, "Is there an outside world?" The important thing is, "Is the outside world better?"

If I stay here, can I earn back the trust of the Community Leaders? Even if I did, wouldn't I always see the contradictions, always want to make things better and be in a constant battle with those who don't?

But there are some things in the Community that are ugly: Mom losing her babies, Serenity's disappearance, the red light thing, and the many lies that don't make sense. Surely the outside world isn't as bad as this. The thought that Scott's name was circled scares me, too. What has to happen for it to be crossed out?

What would life be like if he were gone one morning? What kind of life would Mom have, then?

I feel I'm looking down a path that splits in two directions, knowing that these paths will never join back together, not ever. Will I comply with the Community or find answers to my questions? The familiar or the unknown … it can be one but not the other. The thing is, even though it frightens me, I know which choice I've made—and I can't turn back.

My world is upside down
Instead of firm ground beneath my feet
I find myself underwater
Past the lakeshore dock
Past the lovers in the rowboats
Past the fishermen who reel and net what swims close to the surface.
No, I am beyond them
Deep below, in the murky deep.
And Dad
I know you're out there, too
Somewhere
But you keep playing the game
That we're not here
Not underwater
Not flailing our arms.
The pressure on my lungs builds
And is only relieved by the sucking in of water
And as I do it, I realize that you're doing it too
Somewhere
But you keep playing the game
That we're not out of air
Not drowning
Not longing to be saved.

9

Friday, August 13, 2021

The next morning, I awake to the decision I've made. I know that it's not just a decision for me; others will be affected, unfortunately. Either way, if I do something—or not—others will be affected.

I dress quickly. Into my bag, I pack a hat to cover my head, and then take it out again. Nothing will help cover my boy hair. Although I'm nervous about going to school, my thoughts turn to Anna. I hope she's there today. Maybe Scott and I can get to school early to find out.

But Scott keeps pace with the dragonflies as they circle the lane, and he somehow collects every interesting pebble on our walk to school.

"I can't wait until Mom is better," he says.

"Me, too." I'm distracted, thinking about where on Community land I might find a landing area. I look down at the base of my thumb, still slightly tender but no longer inflamed. That salve really helped.

"She's a better cook than you." Scott giggles loudly at his joke.

How can cargo planes travel past the Community without anyone hearing them?

"Haven't you noticed I'm not asking questions anymore?" he asks loudly.

"You just did," I tell him.

A couple of steps later, I realize I'm walking alone. I turn around.

Scott is in the middle of the road, ten feet back, arms crossed, mouth all in a pout. He reminds me of Misha in the library when she didn't enjoy the way I was reading.

I stride to where he is, take his hand, and pull him gently to a walk. He resists me at first, but then softens and starts skipping again. A thought comes to me.

Scott has lost Serenity, his friend. Even if he hasn't realized it yet, he will hear rumors today, for sure. It's been four days since she disappeared.

How will he react? Will he be afraid that others will disappear?

"I'm sorry, Scott," I tell him, looking at him.

"It's okay," he says. "I wanted to tease you about your cooking."

I tickle his rib, then bend to look under his hat, into his eyes.

"We'll always be together. No matter what happens."

"Even when you're married and you have your Life Role?" He looks at me, eyes wide.

"Yes. I'll need you to come make pancakes every morning for my fifteen children," I say with a wink.

"I enjoy pancakes," Scott says, with a grin. Then his face clouds over. "We'll always be together? Promise?"

What if this is the last question Scott ever asks of me?

I swallow hard. I don't know how this all will end, but I know that he needs reassurance now, to make the awful days ahead of him better.

"Yes," I say, standing up, pulling him to keep walking. "Everything will be at peace in the end." If only I could believe that.

I look at my brother.

His little brow furrows. "Okay. But it's not nice to mumble."

How long did Father tell Mom the ear would take to recover? Will Scott's teachers notice his plugged ear?

Anna is not in the schoolyard when we arrive. As it turns out, we're there just minutes before the bell, not really early at all. And Eric is not at our meeting spot, either, as I secretly hoped.

I kiss my brother on the cheek. "Love you," I whisper into his good ear.

I watch him walk away, and then I head over to the Girls' Building. The warm feeling in my heart dissipates like August dew. Girls point at me, at my short hair. I hear one say, "You're walking the wrong way. The Boys' Building is over there."

I look over at the cornfield, wishing I was a hundred leap-strides into it, surrounded by different kinds of ears.

Brother Michael is at his desk as we come in.

"Good morning, Katherine," he says.

"Good morning, Brother Michael."

At first I think he's just polite, but then I remember that he's singling me out because I missed school. I approach his desk as Sister Margaret comes in and she meets me there, too, arms crossed. I catch a whiff of her aroma: peppermint and sweat.

I lower my head, as is expected of me, and study my dusty brown shoes, noting that one of the laces is untied. This makes me think of Eric. *Eric, his curly russet hair against my hem, tying my shoe.*

"I'm sorry I was absent yesterday. My Mom was unwell and my brother is recovering from an ear infection. I was needed to assist them."

"We know." Sister Margaret says, her lips pursed, the melody in her voice gone.

I panic under Sister Margaret's scrutiny. She seems to read my mind.

"Yes, Katherine. Father always lets us know the medical status of our students and their families."

Brother Michael continues. "We know about Scott's ear infection and your Mom's ongoing issues. But we were concerned that you didn't come to school, especially as it followed your second warning."

Sister Margaret sharpens his point. "Father didn't mention that you had health problems when you were in to see him on Tuesday, so naturally we might conclude you stayed home because you were embarrassed. If it was a reflective day, and you're ready to refocus on your Community, your selfish thoughts at an end, then the purpose was served. If however …"

My shoes go out of focus. I feel trapped … cornered. I'm aware that every other set of eyes in the room is looking at my naked neck. At this moment, I'd say anything to be dismissed.

"I wasn't sick. I was taking care of Mom and Scott so that Dad could work in the hay fields in the afternoon," I explain, even though the Manifesto cites the importance of children going to school so parents can work.

I can't tell them that Dad kept me home because he thought I was sick. Dad thought I was.

Guilt settles in as I finish my sentence. A fine daughter I make. Dad lets me stay home and I imply that he's a Community Rule breaker to my teachers. But Dad can take care of himself, right—especially as he is a Community Leader?

My teacher surprises me here.

"I guess if your family was focused on serving Community needs, your absence is acceptable," says Sister Margaret, the singsong back into her voice.

My mouth opens and I meet her eyes. She's watching me, trying to sketch me in her mind. Is her surprising leniency an example of what happens to kids whose parents are in leadership?

Brother Michael looks to Sister Margaret, then to me. "We hope your conversations with Father have clarified a few things for you. We expect to see a rapid improvement in your attitude."

Sister Margaret nods and narrows her gaze at me.

Or else ... what?

"Yes, Brother and Sister," I say and return to my desk, my face red-hot from the eyes that follow me. I find my seat, careful not to trip on my shoelace.

Anna comes in then, her face flushed as if she has been running, her eyes studying the floor. She takes her place next to me, but accidentally knocks over my knitting needles. She mutters an apology, then drops her writing box. The ink and pens clatter on the wood floor, echoing through our classroom of curious and amused onlookers.

"My hands ... sweaty from the heat ... so clumsy," she explains.

"I'm so glad to see you," I tell her, exhaling loudly, smiling.

Then, she looks at me—my hair—and stares, at first with wonder, then horror.

"In the cornfield," I promise.

The last few days have been hard on Anna. Besides the puffy lids and the sloppy uniform, there are dark circles under her eyes. I doubt she has had much sleep.

Sister Margaret and Brother Michael begin with greetings and announcements. I squeeze Anna's hand—and find it's cold and limp, not sweaty and hot as she just said. I look at her and she bites her lip, sniffs, and blinks. Then she pulls her hand back to hide away a sliding tear.

Brother Michael has us continue our Home Skills knitting projects, in preparation for winter uniform distribution, and I complete the rim on a child-size, beige woolen cap. The thing is, whenever I do something mindless like this with my hands, it seems to focus my senses more keenly on whatever else is going on around me.

But it's not Eugenia, Prudence, or the others who interest me. It serves me well that they must shun me; I have no wish to ever speak to them again. It's Anna I'm worried about—and she's not coping well this morning.

Sister Margaret calls Anna up to Brother Michael's desk. They talk in hushed tones. Anna's head drops; I think she is crying. She shakes her head and her black, curly hair swivels on her shoulders.

Then Sister Margaret stands in front of Anna and gets her to close her eyes. She puts both palms on either side of Anna's forehead, smoothing out the tension from her forehead, from her eyebrows. And I know exactly what Sister Margaret's voice chimes, while she caresses Anna's forehead, because she has spoken these words over me many times.

"What is, is. We don't push nature; we cannot rush a harvest. Do not resist what is, what must be. Accept what is. Release the burden of your individuality. Release for peace."

Sister Margaret's voice rises slightly and I hear her final words before Anna is dismissed to sit down.

"No more selfish absences, Anna. It's time to focus back on your Community."

Are our teachers going to pretend that Serenity never even existed? Father didn't even do that. He visited the home to acknowledge that there was a loss.

I make a fist and bite my lip. How dare they?

A year ago, when I entered Level Ten, I overheard Mom tell Dad that Sister Margaret is unhappy in her marriage and that she works long hours so she won't have to go home to her husband, Brother William, not until late at night. Right now, I'm glad that Sister Margaret's home life is miserable; she should know exactly how Anna feels.

Anna sits down next to me and pulls down coils of her hair. She hides behind them, but I still hear her sniffles.

Brother Michael announces that he's coming around to check our knitting progress. Anna has left her project at home and so must cast-on from the beginning.

We're dismissed for lunch. I head straight outside and Anna follows me into the schoolyard. A few yards away, closer to the Boys' Building, I see Eugenia ... talking to Eric.

I catch my breath. He's here! I assumed he was haying.

Eugenia picks out my gaze and, when she sees me, hooks her elbow with Eric's. He nods at her, blushing, and his eyes travel over her shoulder to where he sees Anna, and ... me. He shakes his head, looks quickly away, his eyebrows knotted.

My heart falls then, falls further than I thought it could. I stride faster to the cornfield, blinking angry tears, swatting back corn leaves that slap my face. I yell to Anna, who is a few paces behind, not caring that the questions tumble out.

"You know Cowbirds, right, the birds that follow cows and horses, eating up grub as the sod turns? They lay eggs in other birds' nests. After they hatch, the Cowbird hatchlings push all the other babies from the nest so they alone can be fed well by the adult birds. Does the Cowbird remind you of anyone we know?"

Anna grabs my arm, her eyes frantic, wild.

"I have a sister. Her name is Serenity. I'm going to find her again. I promise you that. I have a sister. Her name is Serenity. I'm going to—" she implores and then collapses on her knees in tears.

"Hush," I tell her, without really thinking.

Her eyes pop open, a jolt of defiance in them. "I will not!" she shouts.

I kneel next to her and she weeps into her hands.

"I'm sorry," I say, my hand on her thin back. "I'm so sorry for what your family is going through," I say. Then I think of Scott. "I can't imagine it."

"I guess I'm not supposed to talk about Serenity. But how can I just forget her, Katherine?"

Even amid the emotion, I'm surprised. Anna never talks with questions.

"Father told us yesterday that he no longer holds any hope of finding Serenity … that we should accept what has happened and move on. None of the search parties have found so much as a footprint. And the dogs only found Serenity's scent near our house and the school. So how can I accept what has happened when I do not know what that is? What happened to my sister?" she cries, pleading with me.

She searches my face, and then continues. "We shouldn't burden other people in the Community with the past or our problems. That's what Sister Margaret and Brother Michael said when I came in late this morning."

"Ridiculous," I say, shaking my head.

Anna nods, cries some more, and, after a few minutes, runs out of water. She sits there, dazed and exhausted. She is like an oil lamp without any oil.

There is so much I wish I could confide to Anna but I don't know where to begin. Maybe if I get her thoughts off Serenity for the moment, it would be a respite for her mind.

"Scott got an ear infection two days ago and my Mom lost another ..." How much can I tell her? "Mom has been sick and I stayed home yesterday to help. I missed school yesterday because—"

"Try explaining three days," Anna blurts out, and then starts to cry again. It appears that not talking about Serenity upsets her more.

"You haven't been sleeping," I observe.

"Mom cries all the time. I try to comfort her and my father but I'm so exhausted and upset myself. And then there's the housework and my brothers and sisters. My older sister brings the baby over and tries to help, but it's never ending. The little ones don't understand; they're still hungry three times a day."

"But you aren't," I say, noting her missing lunch bag.

"No. I can't imagine life ever being normal again—forget about perfect."

We're more alike than you know. I recline in the dirt row, looking up through the full green corn stalks for any patches of blue sky.

Anna wonders at my view and lies beside me, her feet near my shoulders.

"So many obstacles to our seeing the sky, what's beyond the field … but it's still there," I say, "Even if we can't prove it from right here."

An insect crawls near my collar and I sit up, reaching to flick it away. Then I open my bag for my lunch and offer my sandwich to Anna.

She shakes her head, still looking up. "So peaceful," she says. "I think I could nap right here all day—if only I could."

I take a few bites of Mom's rye bread and cheese.

"Father comes over every day," Anna tells me.

"I think I hate him," I blurt, then cover my mouth with my hand. Why can't I control my words?

Anna doesn't hesitate. "Me, too. He should've been able to save her."

Save Serenity? What does she mean?

I drop my lunch and take Anna's shoulders. "What are you talking about? Tell me."

Anna pulls in a deep breath. "Serenity was sick a lot this spring." She looks at me. "I didn't tell you. We thought it was the flu or a growth spurt that made her so tired. She would muster energy for school, but at home, she'd just sleep. Father started regular nutrition treatments with some kind of needle injection. He said she would be better after a few weeks."

Anna exhales. "We believed him. But then she started developing some horrible symptoms: her hair fell out in clumps; she bruised easily; and she was never hungry."

"I … I never noticed," I admit. How could I miss these changes?

"Mom was always careful to braid her hair in a way that covered her bald patches and when that became impossible, Father gave her a wig. You wouldn't have noticed this because the primaries wear sunhats in the summer. One day, Mom brought Serenity to see Father and he said it was time to stop the treatment. We assumed that she was better."

I wait, holding my breath.

"Five days later … she disappeared."

So there is a connection with the retinal scores and the disappearance. I didn't just jump to a crazy conclusion. This is proof!

"Mom is convinced that she will never see Serenity again, but I can't give up. I don't understand why Father has been so calm. At the beginning, he should have called on Remote for everyone to check their barns, to gather search parties. Even now, it's not too late … it's just summer—she could still be okay if she just wandered off. Though I don't understand why she would leave in the middle of the night. It's unlike her to get lost … and she doesn't sleepwalk; she's such a deep sleeper." Anna's voice trails off, back into her wonderings.

I listen to Anna's anguish, knowing there's so much I want to tell her; so much that might give her answers—but no comfort. Deep down, I know it wouldn't be right. Two risked futures won't help us find truth any faster. It'll just double our chances of being caught.

"Anna, there is something wrong with the Community," I say, finally.

She takes my hand and grips it hard.

"You've been trying to tell me, but I wouldn't believe it. No one else talks like we do." Her voice is hollow and small like a little girl's, like Serenity's.

Our conversation is as serious as night.

"What happened to your hair?" she whispers.

"Failure to reverence Father; second warning. Anna, I've been researching things and I've found a trail. I have to follow it, have to find some answers that might lead to Serenity."

Her eyes widen. "Can I go with you?"

She's in earnest but so depleted. I look at her, sitting in the dirt, red-faced and exhausted. Wouldn't it be wonderful not to be alone anymore?

"No," I say, and she nods.

"Promise me that if anything happens to me, that you'll remember this moment and all we talked about. Remember that I've got it written down in my secret book. It's hidden below the false bottom of my writing box."

Anna looks at me, frantic again. "You're not going away, too … are you?"

"No, no," I say to calm her. "Now, just remember … my purple writing book; you'll give it to my dad, right?"

"Yes, writing box, purple book … wait. Your dad lets you have color?"

It seems an odd thing to ask; so strange, I almost break the tension with a laugh.

"My dad works as hard as anyone in the Community," I tell her. "He got that Role for a reason, though I'm not sure how much of the Manifesto he disobeyed to earn it." I'm suddenly curious. "Do your parents follow the entire Manifesto?"

"Every word," Anna says, her eyes searching mine.

I know now Anna would do anything for me. And it's nice for a minute just to enjoy this. I have a best friend who knows and trusts me. I can never be alone again, even if we *are* separated.

"What's going on?" Anna asks, interrupting my thoughts.

"I'm trying to piece together all the things that don't make sense, like a puzzle, to find out what the truth is."

Her brow wrinkles. I wish I hadn't even told her this much.

"Are you in real trouble, then?"

Our eyes meet and she knows without my saying a word.

"I wish I could help you, but it's all I can do to face the quiet of each night. Coming to school was so hard."

"I know." I see. I hear.

"Find my sister," she says, her bottom lip quivering. Anna's shoulders slump to hug her knees. She rocks back and forth.

This glimpse into my best friend's nightmare motivates me to pursue my new questions, not just ponder them. Maybe Serenity is alive somewhere *through the sky*. Maybe there's a place where Scott and Mom will be safe and Serenity can be with Anna again. It's my dream, but it has nothing to do with perfect.

I hug Anna. For the first time in a long time, I feel understood. For the first time in days, I feel with undeniable certainty that I am doing the right thing.

Revisiting my old primary classroom today
I found a memory
That I'd forgotten
When I was lonely and teased as a child.
I remember thinking back then
That time went so slow
And I wondered
Who I'd be when I was older
And who I was then.
I remember feeling overwhelmed.
But here I am
In a small room
With small windows
A place where smaller minds
Teased me
Believing I'd never be
Who I am now.

10
Friday, August 13, 2021

On the way home from school, I walk with Scott through the cornfield. I'm looking for the metal box with the note in it. I want to check the exact wording and keep it with me in my purple book. Perhaps there's another clue in the wording to hint at a landing area.

Scott is quiet this afternoon and I wonder about his ear. Has he heard anything about Serenity?

I think about my talk with Anna and note similarities between Scott and Serenity. Serenity had a medical problem; she was given medicine, which Father told her would help. Father stopped the treatment and five days later, she disappeared. Her retinal scores are circled and crossed out. Scott's name is also circled; he has a medical problem, was given medicine, and Father suspects he may lose his hearing.

There aren't any children in the Community who can't hear or have lost clumps of hair ... none that I know of. In fact, there aren't any children with any kind of visible health problems.

Will Scott disappear five days after Father stops his treatment? What if I haven't found the landing area by then? Scott catches up with me. He's worried about something; I can see it all over his face.

Is my brother losing his hearing?

I whisper into his right ear. "Scott."

He turns around. Our walk has made him cranky. "No playing, Katherine," he says, whining. "I don't feel well."

"In your ear or …"

"I'm tired—and in school, Terence was talking about Serenity and he said she's not ever coming back to school and that made me so mad, I kicked Terence in the leg and then I had to sit in the corner all afternoon. I tried to tell my teachers that Terence was telling lies about Serenity but they wouldn't even listen one bit!"

So the rumors have drifted down to Level Two already. What should I tell him? If I say that she's coming back, it will hurt again when he finds out the truth. Can he handle the truth? He's only six. He should know but I decide not to tell him anything just yet, unless he asks me directly, and even then I don't know what I'll say.

"Almost there," I tell him.

He grumbles, so I carry his bag for him.

I think back to his hearing problem—if he even has one. I tiptoe up to his left ear.

"Scott." No response. "Scott!" No response.

I imagine life without my brother and can't breathe.

I move to try this test again, feel a tugging at my foot, and then, suddenly, I'm on my face in the dirt. Something is poking into my shin and my elbow stings. Scott keeps walking, but I'm more upset that he didn't hear me fall than I am over my clumsiness.

"*Scott*!" I yell, frustrated. He turns around and runs to me. He doesn't look concerned, only annoyed. I guess he thinks I'm still playing. I roll over and examine my leg. I tripped over an old root.

Scott helps me up. I try to brush the dirt off my uniform and rub my shin.

"I want to go home *now*," he says, his hands on his hips.

"Just a few more steps," I tell him.

"No!"

"Please, Scott. It's important. I … lost something out here." We come to the place where I think the box is. "Rest here," I tell him, putting our bags down.

He lets his body flop to the ground, half exhausted, half angry. I crouch down and start crawling around on my hands and knees.

Why am I so obsessed with finding this box? It's not like it will change anything I've discovered. I try to remember why I'm out here in the cornfield when I should be searching elsewhere for the landing area. And why am I dragging Scott along? I should've brought him home, first. Yes, but Dad would probably need me to stay and fix dinner. I stop and scratch my head. Where was that box?

I'm afraid and I don't know why. I start crawling back to Scott—but on the way, I find the box. It's just as I left it, mostly buried with one corner peeking out. I dig with my fingers to free it, not caring that soil goes under my nails.

Why go through all the trouble of sneaking around the Community—of finding the landing area—if all you're going to do is just write a note? Why not do more?

But maybe the note writer did do more. Maybe he or she is similar to me—hungry for truth and willing to do everything to find it. I open the lid carefully—and gasp.

There is nothing inside. The note is gone! I drop the box as if it is a rotten apple. Was the note all in my imagination? Am I going crazy? What's going on?

I can't think straight. I feel angry, then afraid, all in seconds. A hundred scenarios play in my mind, as if I'm watching myself on Remote.

Scott and I should leave right away. I run towards him but remember that I forgot to bury the box. Hands shaking, I put the lid back on the box and arrange it in the dirt as it was. After one last look, I approach my brother. He's asleep, lying on his right ear, using my bag for a pillow.

I feel like shaking him to get up, grabbing his hand, and running all the way home. I stop myself; I can't do that. I have to stay calm. It's going to be impossible to explain to Mom why I'm covered in dirt as it is, never mind why I made Scott run home.

I stare at him, sleeping so peacefully, and I feel … alone.

Who watches over me? Protects me? Who cares for me the way I care for Scott?

My parents may care, but they don't know me as I want to be known. And I don't know them, not really.

I think of the Planet Keeper, and how wonderful it would be if I was fully known … and accepted. It would be breathtaking to be *that* loved.

And at this moment, I don't believe the Community is alone in the world like a solitary island. Someone else cares. Someone else must be out there. Is it the Planet Keeper who gives me peace in these moments of panic?

I take a deep breath and call for Scott to wake up. He doesn't respond.

Scott is losing his hearing; Father's suspicions are right. What's the next step? A referral? What *is* that?

I feel angry again and protective, as if Scott were my son, not my brother, as if it were my responsibility to save him. I nudge his shoulders. He protests but I pull him to his feet.

"Wake up, Scott," I yell, louder than necessary. "Let's go home."

I pull Scott by the hand from the cornfield onto the road that leads to our farmhouse. Scott is still half asleep while I thrash about like a crow in a cherry tree net. After all, four days ago, the note was in this field and now it's gone. I keep thinking about that—even more than how we can solve Scott's hearing problem or how I'm going to find Serenity.

Did Father hide this note in the cornfield to shake out dissidents? Did Brother Michael or Sister Margaret tell him that Anna and I like to play and hide amongst the stalks? It seems unlikely to me. It would be crazy to have a tiny trap in such a huge area. Besides, Anna and I don't have a specific place where we play here, and we've never seen anyone else in this massive field.

I don't know much about Brother Jake, the cornfield farmer. His kids finished school before me and his grandkids aren't school age yet. Did he write the note?

Then I have an idea. Maybe the airplane landing area is close to Brother Jake's farmhouse. Maybe he heard a shipment come in. It couldn't have been during the day or others would've seen or heard it, too. Brother Jake, or the note writer, must've heard the airplane at night. No other Community workers have houses beyond the isolated Agriculture Areas, so if anyone was going to hear aircraft, it would be a farmer.

Maybe Brother Jake is just like me; he has to write stuff down for it to seem real. Maybe he just hides his writing inside a metal box instead of a secret color book.

This is all coming together, finally making sense. There is just one little thing that's still bothering me. Why would Brother Jake hide the note in his field? Why not bury it near his house with a marker on top? Domicile inspections are rare, and a formality, never extensive.

I keep my writing with me always. But it doesn't make sense that Brother Jake wrote the note and hid it in his own field so far out. The more I think about this, the more I realize that the note writer is not Brother Jake. It must be a farmer from a neighboring field. It makes the most sense that the note is a warning of some kind, one rebel farmer to another.

On one side of the cornfield is a fallow field and the other neighboring field belongs to … Dad?

> *By the steps*
> *I find*
> *Whittled and sanded*
> *A wooden figure of a bird*
> *That Dad has carved for Scott.*
> *Later*
> *I see Dad's hands*
> *Callused*
> *Rough*
> *And bandaged.*

11

Friday Afternoon, August 13, 2021

My mind is sprinting when we reach the house. I'm thinking about the possibility that Dad wrote the note in the cornfield. Could it be true? Has Dad seen the *outside come through the sky*?

I open the door to our house. Mom and Dad are holding hands at the kitchen table. They don't mention how late we are getting home, although I see Mom look at my dirty uniform. Scott runs to hug them both. I think he is relieved, as I am, to see Mom up and looking better. After the arguing I've overheard, I'm glad to see my parents back to their loving ways. I drop my book bag and give them a hug, too. As I pull away, Mom's eyes meet mine.

"Thank you for the help," she says, a tear on her lashes. "You took on a lot of additional chores without a word of complaint."

I look at Dad but he is looking down. One of his strong hands gently squeezes my brother's shoulder, the other picks at bits of twig and dirt from Scott's hair. Is Dad glad for my help, too?

Dad's blue eyes are gray as a stormy sky and he has new wrinkles around his eyes, on his forehead.

I study Dad's face: brown moles, one on his cheek, a few on his neck and rough beard stubble, mostly black, though with a sprinkle of white all over his cheeks and chin. I see his big ears and wide lobes, see the matted black hair partly tucked behind his ear. I smell his sweat, an old clothes smell mixed with newly cut wheat. I can tell just by standing this close to Dad that part of his field is swathed and that he's likely thinking of how to turn the ground before the end of the month so he can seed a crop of winter wheat. One part of his field is cut, though he has many more parts to go.

"It's backbreaking work," I've heard my dad mutter many times. Once he said, with a deep laugh—it's been so long since I've heard that sound—that his favorite part of farming is Snow Break.

I am drawn to this mystery man, but he cannot be known. He looks away, over Mom's head, out the window somewhere. Who are you, Daddy?

Maybe if I start talking, he'll open up, too; maybe he'll become transparent if I lead the way.

I open my mouth and take a deep breath. I want to talk openly about what's going on in the Community. My parents need to know that Scott is in danger. Do they know about Serenity? Do they know about *genetic complications*? I open my mouth but then close it.

"I'll set the table," I say instead, giving me time to think this out.

"You'll change your clothes first," Mom tells me.

"I tripped," I explain before I head upstairs.

I wonder if family relationships have always been like this, even before the Ecological Revolution, with so much left unspoken between a parent and child. I wonder if my parents just now fought the urge to ask, "Where were you after school? Why are you covered in dirt? How did you scratch your shin? Why do you seem upset this week? Have you been crying? What's on your mind?" Somehow, I think they do.

As I'm pulling dishes from the cupboard, I'm glad I shut my mouth. My parents would be frightened if they knew where my plans are headed, especially since they have no idea where my thoughts have been.

After dinner, I play chess with Scott to keep him from watching Kids Hour on Remote. I don't want Father to find out that there's a problem with my brother's hearing. As I watch him move his bishop, I realize that I have only two days left before the next shipment. I'd rather be up in my room, alone, thinking. Should I let Scott win now or make him work harder for it?

"Check," he shouts as Dad comes into the room.

"So happy to win," Dad comments, tousling Scott's hair.

"Pardon?" Scott says, louder than needed. He's been loud the whole game.

"I said, you always want to win," Dad repeats a little louder.

"When?" Scott shouts.

"Win, not when," Dad shouts back, his face now lined with worry. "I hope you're okay, Scott."

"What?"

Dad crosses his arms and looks baffled.

Scott sees this and says, "My ear is all plugged up."

Is that what it feels like to lose your hearing? Does Scott know?

Dad leaves the room and comes back with Mom. She smoothes Scott's hair around his ear and looks into it.

I bite my lip, knowing that if my parents realize the problem, Scott will be going back to see Father.

I move an obscure pawn and Scotts yells, "Checkmate!"

"Maybe you still need your medicine," Mom says. "I hoped your infection would be gone by now." Then she turns to Dad. "Father said: one dropper, half-full, twice a day, for five days *after* the symptoms disappear. It's only been four days since Tuesday."

Dad smiles then, the first time I've seen today.

Don't my parents realize that Scott's hearing seems to be diminishing despite the medicine? Was the medicine just for the pain?

Mom puts the dropper in my brother's ear as he makes the winning move. He smiles the biggest smile I've seen in days.

"One more game," he shouts.

I look to Mom and Dad. They shrug.

"Okay," I say, fighting a wave of reluctance. I think of Anna and what she might give to play one more game with Serenity.

I'm tired the next morning. I lie in bed, half asleep, waiting for Scott to come and wake me up for school. Then I realize, it's Saturday. I jump out of bed and open the drapes. The weather is slightly overcast but it's still going to be a hot one.

I have to find the airplane landing area today. The shipment is tomorrow. I dress and go downstairs. After my chores, I'll ask Mom if I can go for a walk alone.

I'm scrubbing the floor in the kitchen while Mom hangs laundry on the line. I think about going *outside through the sky*.

Do I have the courage? What if the outside world is horrible and I can't get back? Has Dad really seen the *outside come through the sky*? What if I've followed the wrong clues all along on the wrong trail?

Mom comes in as I'm finishing the floor. "Well, we're about done. We really worked hard today."

It's been five or six hours of intense housework in preparation for the upcoming Harvest Break, when the older kids in school will all be working with adults in the Community, preparing for winter, and there won't be any time or energy to see to our own house. I've been trying to work fast and hard so I'd have time later to go exploring. I rest against the counter, my short hair soaked to my scalp.

"Your hair curls when it's short and wet," Mom tells me. "It did that, too, when you were a baby, back when it was all just growing in. You were bald until you were a year, and even then, the hair at the bottom of your neck flipped up—there was nothing on the top."

"I didn't know that," I tell her. Does Mom miss that there is no one to tell her about when she was a baby?

Mom pulls a dish towel off some rising bread dough. I wash my hands and help her shape the dough into the pans.

"No, Katherine. You're done. I want you to have some time to enjoy this gorgeous summer day. This could be your last chance at a break before you get your Life Role."

I take a handful of rye flour and spread it over the counter.

"Not yet. I want to help you. Then we'll both have time," I say.

She's quiet for a moment. "Thank you," she whispers.

"You still need to rest, Mom," I tell her.

She looks at me with a strange face, as if she thinks I can read her thoughts. "You sound just like your Dad."

Mom puts the bread pans under the dish towel so the dough can rise again. "I was going to lie down for a few minutes anyway."

"It's not like an illness; it takes time," I say, and then bite my lip, wishing I could take this back. Am I an imbecile? Now she's going to know that I know.

Her mouth pops open and she stares at me.

I can feel my face turning red. "It's similar to when you had the crying sickness before," I explain. "That's all. It takes time is all I was trying to say."

She wipes her hands on her apron and nods, her head down.

I take my apron off, and take hers, too, putting them both into our empty dirty clothes bin. "I'll go for my walk now," I tell her.

"I'm surprised by your energy," she says, distractedly.

"I haven't seen a whooping crane this year yet. It's not summer unless I have."

"Be back by supper," she reminds me, heading up to her bedroom.

From the kitchen window, my eye catches Scott and Dad, heading into the barn. I duck out the back door so Dad won't ask me to take care of my brother.

What was I doing, talking like that to Mom? Deep down, was I trying to tell her I knew what had happened in her body? I shake my head. I know where I'm going: to the end of Dad's field. If he wrote the note, then he must have heard the airplane from our house, and the landing area could be nearby.

Despite the heat, I walk briskly along the narrow road that leads to where the wheat and corn fields meet. This serves as both a divider and a quick path to the back of his field when other Community members come with horses and wagons for Harvest. After walking for more than thirty minutes, I realize that this is no quick path. It is a large piece of land that my father farms alone, and my respect for him grows.

Down the road, for as far as my eye can see, there is an endless expanse of long, wild, prairie grass. The road appears to end there. As I come closer, I see that the road doesn't actually end but forms a dirt T to border the fields on my right and left. This outer road separates the farming fields from the wild grass.

I choose to turn left instead of right so that I'm closer to Dad's field. What if this is a mistake? What if there is no airplane shipment? I'm afraid that my reasoning has been faulty, that I'm wrong or, worse, that I'm crazy. What if I can't save Scott or find Serenity? And now I've lost Eric—all for nothing?

I increase my pace along the road, scanning ahead and to my right as I go. Desperation begins to blow on me like wind over the wheat field. I know I don't have much time before dinner and the back of my newly bare neck feels scorched by the sun.

I approach the area where Dad's field borders with the ranch owned by Brother Joel, our other neighbor. Now what? The road ahead of me continues on and turns slightly to the left.

I want to cry, except I'm too wound up. I start to turn back, but as I do, I notice a small path into the wild grass at about the place where Dad's field meets Brother Joel's ranch. I follow it: the path is only about ten leap-strides long and gets slightly wider as it goes. Eventually, I come to a huge circular area where the grass grows flat.

What caused the grass to be depressed in this one area? And who made this footpath?

I head back for the road, more confused than ever. The circle is interesting but it's definitely not the airplane landing area I'm looking for. A circular landing area contradicts everything Sister Margaret taught me about aircraft.

Besides, the flat area could be anything—a nesting area or a place where Brother Joel trains his horses … except the edges of the circle should be worn with hoof prints and it's such a long way away. If Brother Joel was breaking the foals on his ranch, he would do this in one of the fenced pens near the stables.

All I know is the shipment is due tomorrow and I'm no closer to figuring out anything about it. Scott could disappear before the next shipment in two weeks if I miss this one. Or he could disappear—like Serenity—between shipments. That's a chance I can't take; it would kill my parents. I know losing Serenity is killing Anna.

I retrace my steps back to where Dad's field meets with Brother Jake's. I'm looking for a long piece of land. The road I'm on is too bumpy and narrow for airplane use, so what else is there?

Maybe the shipment airplane lands on a piece of land parallel with this road. If so, I'd never find it unless I adjusted my course by ninety degrees. I should be able to walk straight out through the grass and eventually bump into it. I reach the T intersection where the two roads meet.

With my back to the Community, I walk straight into the grass—ten leap-strides, twenty, thirty, forty … Then I hear a snap, feel a painful buzzing in my arms and legs, and everything goes black.

In my room tonight
I sit
Arms crossed
Too angry to sleep.
Below, I hear Scott laugh
To numbing, muffled sounds
From the Remote
Yet I am here alone.
Wind whistling through the roof
Lantern shadows casting shapes
And me
Turning pages furiously.
My novel about an ideal place
Leaves me hungry.

12
Saturday, August 14, 2021

I hear faint voices around my head, like clouds. I think I'm dreaming.

"… perimeter fencing …"

"… discovered …?"

Someone touches my arm. A prick of pain jars me fully conscious. Terrified, I open my eyes, but can't make out faces, only black shadowy figures. My head feels foggy and thick. Where am I?

I try to sit upright but every muscle aches in protest. My fingers feel grass and I clench my fists to help me get my bearings. One shadow looms closer and pushes me back, firm. I recognize the voice when it speaks: Sister Margaret.

"Katherine, you've had an accident—but you're going to be okay."

How did she find me? I remember. I was walking deep into the grass past Dad's field. Who are these other people with her?

My eyes try to adjust to the late afternoon sunlight behind the dark figures. I recognize features of Father, and then later, Brother William, my teacher's husband. He stands there, arms crossed, brows furrowed, and bites his cheek. Father bends down and rubs at his forehead.

Panic drills in like a needle and the fog lifts from my brain. Am I about to disappear? Again I try to sit up, ignoring the pain. This time no one stops me. I look ahead and see the T intersection between the wheat and cornfields, where two horses and a wagon wait nearby.

Father turns to put something into his medical bag: a syringe. A thousand questions hit me then, like a summer hail squall. Did I just get a needle? What was it for? Is this similar to what happened to Mom?

My chest feels heavy then, as if Scott is sitting on it. Is this what dying feels like? Father turns around and stares at me, choosing his words with care. "I need to speak with Katherine alone, please," he says, finally.

"Of course, Father," Sister Margaret answers, with a head yank at her husband. They back up for a few steps, then turn around and walk towards the horses.

"What happened, Katherine?" Father asks, a muscle in his cheek twitching.

I try to speak. My tongue feels heavy and the words from my brain all jumbled. "I … w … was … walking." My tongue is slow but my brain races on ahead. Of course I can't tell him why I'm here. I have to think of another reason.

Father motions with his hands, indicating the expanse around us. "Walking out here?" he says with a forced chuckle. "Whatever for?"

"W … walking alone … thinking."

He looks away, clenches his teeth, and forces a swallow, as if he has a sore throat.

"Fought with Scott … needed to be alone." My tongue loosens and the lie tumbles out unobstructed. Is it enough to convince him?

He doesn't let me know if it worked; instead he calls for the others. "Help me put her in the wagon. Let's get her home."

Home!

"I can walk," I insist. I don't want Father to touch me. But when I try to stand, my legs buckle. Father grasps my upper arm, hard, and stops me from falling back. Sister Margaret and Brother William lift me up onto the wagon bed. Holding my breath, I stare straight ahead.

I'm as nervous as the chickens in our coop. I sit up again, this time using the wagon sides for support, though my hands are white from the effort.

"It will be better, perhaps, if you lie flat," Sister Margaret tells me, her lips pursed together as she does when I come in late for school.

"I'm fine," I lie.

"Suit yourself," she says, sitting next to her husband, who holds the reins. Father seats himself on the edge of the wagon bed, dangling his feet off the end. Brother William tongue-clicks to the horses and shakes out the reins.

My sweaty palms slip slightly from where I grasp the side of the wagon. I grip harder to hold on until my arms feel tight and on fire. The horses pull ahead and my body jerks back involuntarily, flopping me on the wagon bed to wallop my head. I lie there a few seconds, dazed a bit, looking up at the blue sky and then at the backs of the others. My head bumps again with every little pothole in the dirt road and I feel so defenseless, almost naked, lying here, surrounded by these people.

Sitting up again, I look out across the wild grass. A trail is flattened, leading to where I had my accident. No doubt, I was dragged back to the place where I woke. But how was I found? What happened out there?

My teeth chatter but not from the cold. And that's when I become aware that I'm being watched. Father has turned his body, so that only his shoulder faces me, but he is studying me from the corner of his eye.

I look down at the grass on my clothes, at the jab of dried blood on my inner forearm. Is that where I got the needle?

"You're a stubborn girl," Father says, fake-smiling again. "Look how you hold yourself up though it pains you. Why don't you rest your body? Here, take my bag for your pillow."

I say nothing, looking away to the ears of almost-ripe corn.

"Hard-headed, independent," he continues. "I've seen that before with Brian, your father. You would get along better in school and with *Scott* if you changed. I want a good, peaceful life for you. Might I succeed at convincing you to trust me?"

"Of course," I say, full of my own frozen pleasantries.

The way Father says my brother's name lets me know he disbelieves my story. Then, for a crazy second, I have doubts about where this wagon is heading, even though we're on the lane that leads right past our farmhouse. Is Father really taking me home? Is this my third warning? Then what?

I'm scared and suck in shallow breaths. Images flood my brain: Mom, Scott, Dad, Trotter, the iron stove, my bedroom ... I want to go home.

The wagon bumbles down the dirt road and comes in view of our house. Dad must hear the horses because he opens the door, hands on his hips.

I'm safe. So relieved, I start to inch my way towards the end of the wagon, my face feeling hot from the effort, the emotions, and my brimming tears.

"Katherine!" Dad yells, striding the distance between us.

Father slides nimbly off the wagon end and takes my hand to steady me. Mom watches from the front door, holding Scott to keep him from running out, too.

"Katherine had an accident," Father explains.

The look of horror on Dad's face breaks me and I start to cry. I hold my arms out to him, as I did when I was a baby, and he reaches for me, too. His embrace feels so good but strange, too. How long since he has held me?

"She was walking in the grass far beyond your field when she met with an unstable air pocket. She was rendered unconscious but should be fine in a day or so. She'll need rest tomorrow but you can send her to school Monday."

"Gracious," Dad cries, hugging me tighter.

"Katherine walked so far because she was upset and needed space to process that terrible sibling fight."

I grip Dad tighter and he doesn't flinch.

"No doubt. You know kids. We must've driven you crazy, Father, all one hundred of us in the Big House. There was always some fight or drama to break up your rare moments of peace. Likely that's how your hair went white so fast."

Dad bends slightly at the knees, preparing to lift me. I rest my head on his shoulder and close my eyes.

"You need help with your daughter," Father observes.

What does he mean?

"I've got her." Dad pulls me closer and collects my limbs.

"I insist," Father says, stepping nearer.

Dad lifts me and faces Father squarely. "Twenty-plus years of manual labor—plowing, sowing, weeding, maintaining this farm, and in every spare minute, working to help others in their Roles. Surely, I can handle my own daughter."

"Can you?" Father's question punctuates the air between us.

Dad and Father lock eyes and I wonder for a crazy second if they might fight.

"We are indebted for your help today, Father," Dad says finally, clearing his throat. "Mary and I are grateful that you were in the area and that our daughter's injuries from the poison air are minor. We certainly apologize for any inconvenience or imposition on your time. Thank you, Sister Margaret, Brother William," Dad says, with a nod in their direction.

And with that, Dad carries me to the porch. I look over his shoulder at the three open-mouthed adults following us with their eyes. I'm just as surprised as anyone. If Dad is this bold, why doesn't he take us all outside *through the sky*?

"We need to talk, Brian," Father calls, just as Dad closes the door.

As if I were a baby, Mom dresses me in my nightclothes. My bed feels so good, so comforting. Then Mom picks up my discarded clothes and throws them into a pile by the door. She opens the drapes for light so she can trim the wick on my oil lamp. It is sunset and the colors warm the room.

"Honestly, Katherine! What you were doing out that far, bird-chasing, I'll never know." She looks at me, searchingly. "You'd tell me if it was a boy with you in the grass. Yes, you would," she concludes from my scowl. "You have to be careful with boys, you know."

There will never be any Eric with me in the grass, at the lake, in our Life Roles. I think of how Eric's affection transferred so quickly to a Cowbird, all because of my hair and my potential loss of a good Role. Is a good Life Role all Eric cares about? Maybe someday I'll believe that Eugenia and Eric deserve each other, but not today. Today I miss Eric.

Mom is a few minutes into her lecture, which I actually don't mind as a favorable alternative to a third warning. "We were sick with worry. You were supposed to be back by dinner and here it is almost dusk."

A light knock interrupts us. Dad opens the door and enters, followed by my brother.

"Katherine!" Scott yells, running to hug me. I sit up, my body less sore than it was in the wagon. After a few tight hugs, Dad pats him on the back.

"Off now, Scott. We need to talk to your sister."

Scott hesitates, then obeys. Mom closes the door behind him, and sits at the foot of my bed. Dad kneels on the floor beside me and brushes my forehead with his hand. Mom fidgets with her cuticles a minute, then stands and crosses her arms.

Will Dad mention the lie I told Father, about the fight?

"On the subject of Life Roles ..." he says, looking at me, "we wonder if any Brothers or Sisters have talked about these with you privately."

"Father made mention of them in my appointment."

My parents exchange a look I don't understand.

Dad says, "There are only so many behaviors the Community Leaders will put up with before they decide against someone and assign certain undesirable jobs, like manual labor." Dad is speaking slower than usual, picking his words carefully. "Two such behaviors they will not tolerate are the use of questions and irreverence towards Father. Another is choosing to ignore the threat of unstable air while walking too far from the Community. You've broken all three of these in one week."

"I didn't know that it's against the Manifesto to go on a long walk," I say, not meaning to argue.

But Dad takes the unintended bait and his voice loses patience.

"A long walk! I wonder if you thought about unstable air before you ventured past the lane," Dad says.

"I promise I *wasn't* thinking about unstable air, Dad," I say. Can I tell him about Serenity? Can we finally talk about the real issues?

He looks a little stunned then, as if he's wondering about my implication.

My mom hears Dad's hesitation and takes over. "We are expected to learn from the Aunts and Uncles who died looking for resources. The air is unstable outside the Community—you proved that today."

Dad gets to his feet and turns to examine the corner of the dresser. "I was twenty at the time. I remember the grief I felt when Uncle Peter, Aunt Rhea, and the others left." Dad turns and points his finger at me. "You're lucky to be alive."

Does Dad really believe this? Doesn't he think it's coincidental that Father found me today so quickly? How did they happen to be out there where I was?

Mom falls to her knees and takes my hands. "Katherine, unless the Community Leaders see a big change in you, I am sure you will have sealed your fate today with what you did." She shakes her head, lifts her hands to her face, and begins to cry.

Dad's stern eyes look for mine. "This week, you have shown a complete lack of reverence for what you've been taught in school. It's likely too late to recover from that now. We were hoping that your life would be different from ours. With your aptitude for learning, I'm sure you could've been a Community Engineer or Medical trainee."

I wanted to work with books with Sister Millie! I bite my lip, trying not to cry. An image of the red-faced, hairnet-wearing, dairy queen Sister Bernie comes into my mind. I can't imagine her bossing me around for the rest of my life.

If my parents were yelling at me, I could respond better, but their continued disappointment stings, like iodine in a deep scratch, and, for the first time, I wish I'd lost my questions years ago. A sedate mind in a good Role—with Eric—might have had moments of wonderful.

"You have to change, Katherine," Dad says. "Stop learning the hard way. I'm going to talk to Father tonight and we'll discuss this again in the morning."

They are going to talk about me. What will they decide?

"Don't say it," Dad says to Mom as they leave.

They go out and close the door.

"She's her father's daughter, that's for sure," I hear Mom say, her voice shrill again as she begins to argue with Dad about bargains, deals, and, finally, I hear, "Just like you."

What does she mean by that?

> *From inside the cornfield*
> *I hear the boys*
> *Playing Kick Ball.*
> *They scream as if they are in pain*
> *But Anna and I know*
> *They are only calling for the ball*
> *To be passed to them.*
> *They remind me of crows*
> *Gathering*
> *Fighting over the last piece of bread.*

13
Saturday Evening, August 14, 2021

I want to scream after them, "What do you mean by that?" Instead, I cry it into my pillow. How am I my father's daughter? Why can't I just behave and submit?

I remember hearing that kind of thing when I was younger, in trouble. Mom would say to Dad, "She's your daughter," as if what I'd done was his fault. Now, Mom speaks as if it's a fact, as if I am my father. How am I like Dad?

I've always assumed I'm more like Mom. There were times when this bothered me, because I've always wanted to be my own person, but something has changed since Mom lost this baby. I feel reverence for her. But like Dad?

He's soft-spoken, quiet, strong, and dependable ... and even though I don't see these characteristics in myself, we must have other similarities, somehow. Father hinted at it, too, in the wagon and during the appointment. He said we were both hard-headed, independent, stubborn, and that we both asked a lot of questions.

I can't prove it yet, but if Dad wrote the note in the cornfield, then he also shares my desire for truth and answers. He is daring and brave, having seen the *outside come through the sky*. Today, he spoke boldly to Father, something I've never seen him do before this week. Dad with his "over twenty years of manual labor … grateful that you were in the area when you were," as if he was telling Father he knew exactly what happened to me in the field. Dad and his manual labor, warning me about manual labor.

Did Dad get his Role because of intolerable behavior as a young man? How did Dad then get invited to be a Community Leader if he was so bad? Did what happened to me today also happen to Dad at one time?

I feel almost sure of it. I wiggle my toes and try to move my legs. The pain is dull and numb; still there, but diminishing. I try to get out of bed, but a knock on the door interrupts me and I scramble to cover my bare legs.

"Come in," I say. Is Scott bringing in the chessboard?

Mom enters with food on a tray. Dad follows her in to help me sit up. He adjusts my pillow to support my lower back and then Mom places a tray on my lap with a plate of green beans, potatoes, and a small piece of salted beef.

"Thank you," I say, my mouth already watering. I hadn't realized how hungry I was.

Dad adjusts the lamp wick to get rid of the flicker and says, "You've been through a frightening ordeal, so make sure you get lots of sleep tonight."

I get an idea. If Dad knows about my "ordeal" and what to expect in recovery, then he must have experienced this, too.

"Dad, the pain is slowly going away," I tell him, my heart beating faster.

He takes the bait. "That's normal. You should be able to walk, no problem, by morning." He turns to Mom. "I'm going to ready Trotter, but I'll be back to carry Katherine to the tub."

So Dad knows.

Mom watches him go, biting her lip, but I'm still in my own thoughts.

Why does Father want to talk with Dad? How does Dad know when I'll be better? He must know what this feels like. So it takes overnight to recover? That long?

Tomorrow is the fifteenth of the month—shipment day—and I still haven't found the landing area. I needed to find it today but failed. If only I could share what I know with Dad. He knows where the landing area is because he's seen the *outside come through the sky.*

But why didn't he do anything once he saw it? And what exactly did he see? He must have discovered the plane as it landed, seen it drop off a shipment and then leave again. If Dad somehow had managed to get *on* the plane, then he wouldn't have been able to return until the next shipment. But since he's never spent a night away from the farmhouse to my knowledge—and certainly never two weeks—I think Dad just *saw* the plane.

"… boiling water for your bath. Katherine, I don't believe you've heard a word I've said," Mom says with exasperation. I've tried her patience to its fullest extent today.

"You're right. My mind was elsewhere. Sorry. Bath day, Saturday."

I look down, and fork some beans into my mouth. Delicious.

"Your face is transparent," Mom tells me. "Your forehead was furrowed in concentration. You must be worried about not being able to walk."

"No," I say, without thinking.

Mom folds her arms and her face wrinkles into a frown. "You should get cleaned up and go to sleep as soon as you can. I am just about to siphon water for your bath."

"Thank you," I say and take another bite.

"Scott's ear infection still hasn't cleared up and the medication seems useless. I'm taking your brother to see Father tomorrow if his hearing doesn't improve overnight."

"No," I say. My fork clatters noisily to the floor and a piece of bean gets caught in my throat. I try to swallow.

I cough repeatedly to try to clear my airway. Mom thinks I am choking and comes over to me, but her eyes are only slightly concerned. I motion that I'm okay.

There must be a way to keep Scott from seeing Father.

"It's just a simple infection," I say, with a shrug of my shoulders. "I really don't see the need to bother Father again. After all, he did say it would clear up in a few days. Perhaps Scott's ear just needs more time."

"He can't hear from his left ear." Mom knows.

I fork some potatoes into my mouth, as casually as possible, though my hand is trembling.

Mom just stares at me, her face reddening.

"Blurting out your opinions on when to take a child to see Father, not listening when I'm talking to you, and walking too far from the Community ... honestly! I don't understand you at all, Katherine."

She turns and leaves my room, sputtering under her breath as she does. "Call Scott to take your tray when you're done eating. Dad will be in shortly to carry you to the bath, though I wouldn't mind so much if he dropped you on your head!"

Dad carries me to the tub, then leaves so I can undress. I stand on my own feet and step into the half-filled aluminum tub of warm water. I sit on the bottom, knees by my chin, the water level at my neck. This position relaxes and comforts me despite the heaviness I feel looming over my heart.

I love my mom and understand why she is mad. I sense her disappointment and wish I could be what she wants—docile, hard-working, and agreeable. But I can't be submissive to ideas that don't make sense, or believe everything I'm told. I can't just pretend that Scott won't disappear. I can't try to have a good life and just forget that a sweet little girl named Serenity used to be my best friend's sister. I told Anna I would try to find Serenity. When I found the note, something changed in me and I can't change that part of me back.

What Mom thinks of me is beyond my control. What I can control is finding the landing area. Tomorrow is the fifteenth of the month. Tomorrow night is when the shipment takes place, but from where?

The landing area isn't parallel with the road or I would've walked right into it. Where else could it be? So much depends on Dad's writing the note, on Dad's hearing the airplane from our house. What if I'm wrong? Then I have nothing to work with, no clues, no chance, and I will have to consider that the landing area is anywhere else around the boundary of the Community. Too scary … I push this thought down deep.

Before the accident, I was measuring, with leap-strides, the distance from the outer road. I remember a snap, the buzzing, but nothing else. Why didn't my lungs struggle if I encountered an unstable air pocket? This is the first time I've wondered this. I should have gasped for breath or felt suffocated—as I did when I was learning to swim in the lake and my head submerged in the water. I was desperate to survive, panicking and flapping my arms. Why don't I remember that same reaction to the unstable air? And why didn't I die if I was deprived of oxygen? Also, shouldn't Father issue an alert if the poisonous air is that close to the Community? It just doesn't make any sense at all that unstable air knocked me out.

And how was I rescued so quickly? Did the syringe make me conscious? Does Father make regular trips along the perimeter of the Community just in case someone—or some animal—has met with bad air? There's something else about this, on the tip of my brain, that I can't quite remember. I think back to the foggy feeling before the syringe. I heard something—voices mentioning something about … perimeter fencing. Fencing? Could I have walked into a type of fence, a sort of boundary? Was Father alerted somehow that the fence was touched in a precise location and that's how he found me, lying alone in a sea of prairie grass?

This is the only option that makes sense: an invisible fence with a warning device.

That would explain how Father found me so quickly and was able to rally the others to help him get a wagon, help him carry me from the fence to where I woke up. I shake my head, astounded at the possibility. I never would've believed it possible if I hadn't read those papers in Father's office.

Perhaps the landing area is secured beyond the fencing. Maybe the power of the fencing is shut off during a shipment. Can I find out by tomorrow night? Tomorrow, the night of the fifteenth, in the darkness, a shipment will arrive *through the sky*.

A terrifying thought occurs to me. The night of the fifteenth at some point becomes the morning of the sixteenth. My heart is beating out of control, as if I'm late for school—only so much worse.

The shipment is on the fifteenth. Is that the evening of the fifteenth or the morning of the fifteenth? The darkest part of the night, in the wee, early morning hours when the whole Community is deep in sleep, is a much safer time to make a shipment than the evening hours leading up to midnight.

The morning of the fifteenth is just hours away. But I can't fully walk yet—or can I?

> *What happens to the unuttered?*
> *Or inappropriate words that are swallowed?*
> *Feelings too raw to write down?*
> *Or questions never asked?*
> *Do they disappear?*
> *Return?*
> *Or explode?*

14
Saturday Night, August 14, 2021

I wash my short hair with lard soap and rinse. Using the wall and side of the tub for support, I try to stand. Carefully, I step from the tub to the mat on the floor and dry myself off. I bend down and pick up my nightclothes. My legs buckle then and I have to grab the sides of the tub to keep from falling.

I dress and slowly move to the door. By the time I get there, I'm exhausted and weak. I lean my head against the door and start to cry. It's not that I feel sorry for myself—this pain is not overwhelming. I'm crying because I can't manage all that I'm feeling. I'm afraid, anxious, scared, and very tired. Am I ready to go *outside through the sky* to find Serenity? Have I the courage to find the truth? What if I fail my brother?

My body crumples on the floor against the door. My tears turn into sobs. I think about the disappointment I am to my parents. I remember Scott chasing Serenity by the swing set—it seems like ages ago now since she was well enough to do that. I let myself go until I'm breathing so fast, I'm out of breath, as if I just ran a race—but then I can't make this breathing stop. This scares me, so I stop think-ing of sad things and try to remember something else—deep red watermelon, noisy crickets, soft yellow baby chicks, and the shaky legs of a brand new foal.

My eyes are sore, my forehead strained, and my whole head throbs. I'm thirsty but feel too weak to get a drink. I rest my head against the door and close my eyes. Please, Planet Keeper, let me be able to walk in time to find the airplane. And then, like a lost child worn out and exhausted beyond worry, I fall asleep.

I awake with a start when I hear a knock at the door. Only a few minutes have passed, I think. Mom calls my name.

Has she heard me crying? I sit up and reach for the doorknob. "I'm still here," I say, trying to cheer my voice.

"You've been in there such a long time," she says, her voice soft.

"I'm almost out. One more minute."

I hold onto the doorknob and use it for support to stand. Splash-ing water on my face from the basin, I look into the looking glass on the wall. My eyes are puffy and red. How long was I asleep? I reach my hand into the tub; the water is room temperature, so it's been a while.

Using the wall for support, I shuffle to the door and open it, expecting to find Mom there, arms crossed. But the hall is empty, so I work my way to my room and crawl into bed. I can walk, sort of. Is it enough?

I think about the next shipment and try to gather my courage. What I have to do tonight is dangerous and, if I get caught, I will receive a third warning. How many warnings did Dad get?

What would it be like to remain here if Scott disappeared? Or if neither of us disappears? Either way, it is a hard life. Mom comes in as I'm thinking this.

"Oh, good," she says. "You're in bed."

I nod.

"Scott is asleep," she tells me, folding my quilt, up near my neck. "You were in the bath a long time."

Is she wondering why I took so long? Did she hear me weep behind the door?

"I feel better now," I tell her, simply.

"Hmm." Mom looks distracted, as if she's thinking about something else. She gets up and tidies the top of the dresser where my hair things are. "Your dad will be home soon."

I look at the back of her head. I wonder if she's noticed my red eyes or knows how confused I am. I wish she could take my questions and reassure me, make me feel safe, like she did when I was a young girl. She can't, though, because this is not about either of us. I think about what Anna and I talked about in the cornfield: there is something wrong with the Community.

Why does Mom pretend that everything is okay? Why does she think that if I just conform to Community expectations, I can have a good life?

Mom finishes with the dresser, then comes over to kiss me on the forehead. "Good night, Katherine. I love you." She leaves the room.

I blink unexpected tears. It's been so long since I've heard her say this. "Oh, Mom," I whisper. I know what I have to do.

An hour after Dad has returned, and the rhythm of the house is back to the deep snores and exhales, I slide out of bed. I test my legs; better, but not normal. I dress warmly with my winter rations jacket, and fill my bed to make it look like I'm there. My bag is packed with my writing box, candles, matches, and a blanket. I don't know what to expect tonight, though I've been thinking for hours about what I should bring. What will I need to go outside through the sky?

I decide to leave a note under my pillow, just in case. It takes a long time to decide what to say, but then I just scribble down my best ideas, though they are far from perfect.

Mom and Dad,

I've gone out through the sky to find Serenity and to save Scott. His hearing loss is likely from the B21 virus and he is about to be referred. Father was involved with Serenity's disappearance—I saw the papers in his office that prove it. I know that Ruth and the others send information to Father. I know about the shipping schedule and the landing area. I know what happened to Mom. Sorry we couldn't talk about it.

Katherine

As I check my room, and re-adjust the stuffed bed, I decide to leave my purple book with all my thoughts and questions under my pillow, too. I creep soundlessly to the kitchen, then wrap some dried fruit, cheese, bread, and a knife into a dish towel. I limp to the door, open and close it with barely a squeak. Before I can change my mind, I'm in the night air, shuffling towards the end of the wheat field.

I'm sure it's about midnight by the time I get to the т at the end of the road, and what would normally take thirty minutes in daytime has taken almost two hours. I crawl into the wheat field and fall in exhaustion, lying with the blanket covering me, my eyes gazing at thousands of stars, my ears attentive to burrowing owls and grasshoppers.

Serenity was right. I see the little stars that move. What kind of star moves that fast in space?

But I hear no other sounds, nothing to confirm that I've chosen the right spot to wait. Later, I decide to explore along the road that borders Dad's field and the wild grass. I make it to where Dad's field ends, near the path with the flat grass and then wait, but still nothing extraordinary happens.

I'm sure now that I'm in the wrong place at the wrong time. I'm tempted to just go home, except I'm so desperate to be right that I don't know *how* to return home, having failed. I nestle into the security and camouflage of Dad's field and decide to stay, at least until dawn when the strength in my legs has returned. The night air is chilly, even with my winter jacket and blanket. Using my bag as a pillow, I rest my head amongst the stalks of wheat, the aroma of soil deep in my nostrils.

After an interminable time in the moonlit shadows, I begin to hear the plodding sound of the hooves of horses. I think my ears are mistaken, or that I'm dreaming—except I think I also hear the clunky metal and wood sounds of a wagon. So, something is happening tonight.

I am more scared than relieved. I had almost resigned myself to a transparent talk with my parents, regardless of the consequences. Eventually, I'm sure I detect voices and crawl on my hands and knees to where I can see the road from my hideaway.

The wagon passes and I hold my breath. In the moonlight, I see Father and Sister Margaret. I look for Brother William, but unless he is lying down in the wagon bed, he's not there. The wagon stops about five leap-strides from me. I'm frozen in fear, afraid to move, afraid to breathe—but they don't move, they just sit there. A few seconds or so later, they resume talking. I pull my knees up to my chest, hugging them, listening intently.

"It's early yet," Father says.

"So what's coming tonight?" Margaret asks him, her voice changed again from how she normally sounds in the classroom. Now she sounds older, tough, determined.

"Scanners, electrodes, replacements of medical stocks, and ..." Father pauses here.

"And?"

"Ruth is sending verification of program funding for the entire term of the newly elected government. Our team has been busy advocating for us."

"Which means?"

"Margaret! Must I explain everything to you more than once? If you're going to replace me, become Mother, you must study and memorize our talks."

Sister Margaret as the new doctor, as Mother? What does he mean? Where would Father go?

"I know. It's just that sometimes I find the terms of your world confusing. You chose to raise me here, remember? Your experiment is the only home I've known."

Experiment?

"Which makes it all the more authentic. You are free from doubt. You will build and protect the only life you have ever known."

They are thoughtful for a minute. I feel a sneeze coming but I plug my nose and breathe in deeply through my mouth.

"What about the Prime Minser?"

"Minister, Margaret, the Prime Minister, the newly elected leader of Canada. He's approved four more years of funding."

Canada? What's funding? There are those words again.

It's weird to hear Father talk to Sister Margaret as if she were a child; so bizarre that in another situation it might almost be funny.

"You were worried?"

"Remember when the crops failed with the locusts but there were always a few more rations available, even though the cupboards were bare in the winter? Well, without funding, famine would be a regular occurrence … but we wouldn't bemoan that so much, compared to other new problems. Imagine intrusions from hunters and tourists, an unprotected fly-zone, an epidemic of a flu virus, or another instance of cancer. Anyway, I don't have to worry about that anymore. What a relief. Four more years of funding."

"But what would the implications be if the election had gone the other way?"

"This isn't the seventies anymore. If people knew about it—I say *if*, Margaret—I'm not sure they would approve. Some would argue that the Experiment results have proved nothing. It doesn't help that the government changes what they want from us every decade. Trudeau fostered an atmosphere for social engineering with a focus on genomes and perfection. His successors during the Cold War needed insight into Communism. After that, it was genetics, but for the last fifteen years, it's all about ecology and sustainability. I don't complain; I keep changing and adjusting our Manifesto, though it is irritating to do so."

Which people? What results?

"But perfection is still possible, Father. I know it, I feel it; we are so close."

"Feelings have nothing to do with it, nothing. Besides, every extraction is a slap in the face."

"Slap in the face?"

"Figure of speech, Margaret, from when I was a boy. Every time we extract someone, we fail. I fail. Regardless of the high number of factors we control, there is always something beyond us."

"Are you thinking about the most recent one?"

"She's fine; receiving more extensive treatments than I could ever give and now likely to live. Still, it seems that no matter what technology I have, there is a need just beyond it, something that I can't fix."

Is he talking about Serenity? Is she alive now only because she disappeared? Was she going to die here?

"But you are brilliant, Father. Your genius will find a way."

"Sometimes I wonder if intelligence is enough. I had the most upsetting conversation with Brian tonight."

Dad?

"Oh, he's easy. He adores his family," Margaret says. "He'll stay quiet for them."

"But he thinks in such an unconventional way. I didn't teach him that. You know I've squelched him to every extent, and yet he still questions, he still fights me. Ever since he was a baby, I've followed every word of advice from the Community Architects. I over-provided unsolicited information, created a loving environment of safety and security with no conflict or danger, had his teachers focus on a literal education—avoiding creative, critical, or inferential thinking—offered distraction and paired him with the woman he pined for, overloaded him with physical work, created the Remote to numb and offer more distraction ... where have I gone wrong here? Am I to believe that it is impossible to design a human who does not question? Is it only pain that breaks the human spirit? I can't believe that."

"Just work on his daughter. Brian will be docile then," Sister Margaret says. "You could negotiate a good Life Role for her in exchange for his joining the Community Leaders."

Work on his daughter? Me?

"There's always his son ..." my teacher says.

Scott? What will she suggest?

Sister Margaret's voice changes here, and she almost sounds whiny, like Eugenia. "It's his own fault, Father. Brian brought it on himself. He always has. He was annoying as a boy. I couldn't stand him. How will he change and listen to me when I'm Mother?"

Father ignores her questions. "But, Margaret, some would say I wrestle against the invisible, something I can never master, the human condition. Some would call me a fool."

Who is some?

"How dare they! You have sacrificed your life for something noble. You, at least, have tried to do something about worldly problems. Your life will not be in vain.

"Some would say that I've created a community without spirituality and a people without souls."

Souls?

"What do those words even mean?" Sister Margaret asks.

"They are irrelevant, fictitious concepts disregarded by many in the world outside. Soon, Margaret, I will let you see the same media I showed the others. You would not believe the problems out there, though."

Problems?

"Thank you, Father. I want to know all you know. I want to even visit outside."

"Never. It would corrupt you."

"Oh," she says, and seems to take a deep breath. "Very well. I trust you."

"I know you do. And you know I only live for my people and would do anything for them. You are a great comfort to me, Margaret, even though I have been tough on you. It is for the benefit of your training. I have so much to teach you and so little time."

"So little time, Father? But you are strong and healthy and—"

"Seventy-five. Most people retire at sixty out there, Margaret. I won't always be here. You must be Mother when I die. You will control the Community Leaders, and Ruth will arrange for your funding and needs."

"Yes, of course." Sister Margaret's voice gets softer and gentler. I strain to listen. "Will you allow the artisans to display their color in a Market?"

"No, and neither should you. It's an expression of the Individual and it's such a slippery slope from personal expression in color and choice to hoarding and greed. This is the problem of the world outside and I will not allow it here. We must stand firm. Many eyes are on us, especially the Ecological Socialists."

"But how to squelch it?"

"Domicile Inspections during Snow Break. That's when we'll catch the dissidents and we'll come down hard on them. We'll make them burn their creations and cut their fuel rations until they do."

"That will work," says Sister Margaret. "Good thinking. Father, what has been the most difficult thing for you?"

"The separation from Ruth, your mom. But you will learn to master the loneliness as I have done."

Sister Margaret is Father and Ruth's child?

"But what will I do about Brother William, Father? You chose him for me, but he's so difficult, so sulky. I just don't think we can be civil anymore."

"Not now, Margaret, it's time."

My heart jumps into my throat. Am I ready to see the *outside come through the sky*?

> Behind the barn I hear Dad
> Chopping, banging, breaking wood
> Intervals of time in between.
> And I wonder
> Will the ax lift again?
> Or is it silent for another day?
> Is the work finally done?
> Or will the man keep toiling?
> I listen
> And wonder why he is silent during dinner.

15
Sunday Morning, August 15, 2021

Father climbs down and goes to the back of the wagon. Sister Margaret follows him. He slides out a long, shiny tube and hands it to her, then pulls out another one and reaches for a box. They walk from the wagon towards the flat, wild grass.

I crawl back for my blanket and bag. The wheat stalks seem to rustle together too noisily. I bite my lip, hoping I haven't been noticed, though it's hard to hear anything beyond my heart thumping up near my ears.

I move to where Dad's field meets the road. I don't see Father or Sister Margaret anywhere, so I cross the road as fast as I can. I crawl into the wild grass for ten leap-strides and lie flat.

And then, farther away, I see powerful, white lights. Those silver tubes must be lights. Are they signals for an airplane? I hear muffled conversation and something else, something almost imperceptible, then something faint, then something I can't describe, getting louder, as if a wild magnitude of horses were moving my way. Is this the airplane?

It gets louder but I feel it before I see it. The whipping wind hurls around me like a winter windstorm, and I stuff my blanket back into the bag to keep it from flapping around. I cover my ears, my palms to my lobes, as tight as possible, and almost get knocked over. I crouch down then, and the wind gets stronger as the noise gets higher, screaming, and more intense. The noise beats with my heart: thump, thump, thump. I look up. Something like a giant metal— and I don't know how else to describe it—dragonfly descends about fifty leap-strides away. The white tube lights mark its sleek, black shape, and tiny red lights—and one green one—mark its actual size. There are two wind makers that spin horizontally on the top and a smaller vertical one at the back.

Father and Sister Margaret run for it, carrying boxes, but I notice they have coverings on their ears and Sister Margaret has her hair tied back. Two men in dark clothing open doors—two in the front and two behind.

So this is *outside through the sky*! Dad saw this!

Father and Sister Margaret receive boxes from the men and stack them on the grass. As they work, efficiently and rapidly, I realize that I don't have much more time. How can I get on this thing undetected?

I panic. I can't do this. Dad didn't. So I can't. I'm just like him, right?

I think of Anna, of telling her that I tried, and that I know Serenity is safe, that I'll go looking at the next shipment. But by then, Scott might be gone, too, snatched alone in the night, taken on one of these insect things alone.

How horrifying that would be for him to endure! Did Father

make Serenity unconscious the way the fence jolted me? Did she wake up in a different place, with strange people?

I imagine Scott would scream and cry for us. How many days did Serenity keep that up? Has she withdrawn into herself and now stopped talking altogether? I can't let that happen to my brother. I will keep my promise to Anna, though this next step terrifies me more than anything I've ever done.

I squat, continuing to examine the ship. I know I won't be able to get in on the side where Margaret and Father are talking to the men. To get a closer look, I work my way around the circumference of the flat grass, away from the light, until I am on the opposite side of the dragonfly ship, alone. As I'm looking, I hear Father yell and it sounds something like, "Last box, Jim?"

I don't listen for the reply. I scramble in, climbing over a seat and onto the floor, as far back into the ship as I can. Tugging into my bag for the blanket, I cover myself, shivering, scared.

Father yells something else but then the doors close. I resist the urge to peek, and just stay on the floor, waiting. A few seconds later, the sound of the machine seems to get more intense, and the front of the ship lifts up. And then I have the strangest experience of my life. It's as if I weigh nothing at all but as if I'm falling, too. The dragonfly ship moves up, at first seemingly unsteady. I clench my teeth. How high will we go? My stomach leaps into my throat and a wave of dizziness hits me. We rise, tilting, lurching.

It's at that moment that I realize I'm leaving the Community and life will never be the same. Will I see my family again? Anna?

I sit up, peeking over the seat and the boxes, to the front of the ship. Two men, the one Father called Jim and the other, sit with their backs to me, facing many little dots and button things. They both wear round objects on their ears and they speak words I can't quite discern. I don't understand how they hear each other either above the rattling noises of the ship.

I move so that my head can hide behind a box and still look out the window. Behind us, I see the two white lights of the landing area and small shadows moving around them. Beyond that, as far as my eye can see, is pitch blackness. Where is my home out there? Is this why the Manifesto insisted on thick drapes at every window, to block the lights Father needed to signal the ship?

My teeth chatter and I can't stop them. I watch the lights grow smaller, still holding my ears as I do. My stomach swirls and rolls. When I can no longer see the markers, I curl back onto the floor, rest my head against my bag, hugging myself under the blanket.

I cry then, biting the arm of my jacket to stop from screaming. I am a prisoner of this ship now, and the sights and sounds are confusing and frightening.

I sit up, drying my eyes. I actually think if I were to scream, the men up front wouldn't hear me. That's how loud it is on the ship. And there's this smell I detest—like a kind of sunflower oil, but heavier—and the air is thick with it. The mat on the floor is gray and made of something I don't know that is rough, and the space is tight, making it impossible to stretch out. Something pokes into my back, my legs cramp, and my ears hurt.

A headache begins and I shiver. The ship tilts, bumps as if I'm on horseback—only so much worse—and it's almost like we're slowly being jarred along through the air. My stomach pitches one last time and I realize I must find a place to throw up. I spread out my blanket and I'm the sickest I've ever been in my life. Then I hurriedly roll the blanket into a ball, to try to mask the stench. Can the men smell it, too, even up there in their seats? I watch their heads, but they don't turn around. My tear-weary eyelids close but it's impossible to sleep; the air along the floor is as cold as an ice sheet over a lake, and I constantly shift to keep one body part from freezing or cramping. Often, I look out the window and see tiny lights below.

My mind races the whole time. Have my parents discovered that I'm gone? What will they say when they read my secret purple book and note? Where will I be when this thing lands?

As the minutes pass, I realize I have a new problem. This is not a quick trip to Serenity. What is my plan when I find her? We can't walk home to Anna now—that's clearly impossible.

When it feels like the ship will never lower back to earth, my ears pop—unexpectedly—and the sound of the aircraft grows more intense. I cover my ears against the splitting sound. There's another rumble and we turn. If a giant was jiggling us in his hand, this is how it would feel. There's a vibration in my chest and I'm shaking all over. I yawn to relieve my ears and try to make them pop again.

Then there's a rumbling, a squeezing, a lowering, and another turn. The ship lifts up in the front again, and I feel it connect with land below. Then the front lowers and turns, moves forward by fractions, and stops. I hide on the floor, the soiled blanket wrapped and pushed under the seat. The whirring slows and I can distinguish sounds now: wa, wa, wa! White light spills into the ship. I tuck my body as tightly as I can into the shadows and away from the boxes.

After a few minutes, the sound of the engine slows and stops. The men talk more, words and details concerning the gathering of their things, the securing of the ship. Finally, the doors close and it's quiet.

I wait a minute, then peek out the window. Bright, blinding lights surround the ship. Where are we? My breath is shallow and excited, my eyeballs overloaded by whiteness.

I see the two men standing in front of a small white building with a shiny, clear door. Beside them is a sort of cart loaded with boxes. Now what? The door opens and the men roll the cart in before the door closes behind them.

I check out the view from the other side of the ship, looking for people, anything. The lights are so bright that when I turn away and close my eyes, I still see them.

After many minutes, now convinced I'm alone, I look for a way off the ship. I crawl over the seat, and over to a door. There is a red label on it that says EXIT. I pull at a lever near the label and the door gives way. I reach back for my bag, and on second thought, for the blanket. If someone found it—and they would soon, knowing how anything putrid can take over a room—they might recognize the blanket from Community rations and launch a search party.

Crawling out, I try to stand. My legs feel shaky, cramped, and asleep. I walk towards the glass door, my bones and muscles sore, but then stop, because it's as if I'm being pulled in circles. I sit down until everything can stop moving.

I close my eyes, waiting for the circles to stop. While I wait, I make my plan. I'll leave the aircraft area, find Serenity while it's still night, and then we'll hide out during the day until I can figure out how to get us home. Maybe we'll have to wait two weeks until the next shipment. If so, we'll need food, water, and blankets.

I puff out my cheeks. This is going to be harder than I thought.

I grow impatient with my dizzy head and crawl to the white building.

When I get there, I discover that the door is forced shut, similar to Father's office cabinets. Somehow Father and Jim know how to open doors that are mechanically fixed.

How did Jim and the other man open this? Is there another door? I hear a clicking sound and the bright lights go off. What did I do? I flatten myself against the small building, afraid to move. My eyes adjust and I see that I'm not in darkness at all but surrounded by thousands of smaller, less intense lights, like unflickering, multi-colored candles far away.

I explore, walking as far as I can in one direction until I come to a metal fence. I peer over it and learn that I am on the roof of a building, hundreds of leap-strides off the ground and surrounded by other enormous giant buildings. On the ground are tiny, noisy, zipping red and white lights that move. The sight makes me dizzy again and I look away, resting my head against the metal fence while I find my balance. I follow the fence, along the perimeter, looking for another door.

I look back at the ship for any clues and see *N525SA* written on it. Up near the front of the ship, there's a label that says Canada and one that says *Sikorsky X2*.

Despair seeps in as I realize there is no other way off this roof and it's just a matter of time before I get caught. Did I come all this way to get stuck here? What would Dad do now? Returning to the only structure on this roof besides the ship, I find a place in the shadows, near the glass door, and wait. I remember a summer day at the lake, in a rowboat when a squall blew in, and I was pelted by rain, soaked, unable to see the shore, blindly paddling for the dock, wildly fearful of lightning. I remember the lost feeling and wondering if my parents would find my body. This is worse because I know they won't.

It's still dark when I'm found. A bright light holds steady in my face, one too blinding to look at directly. A voice speaks, gruff and unwelcoming, and I realize, days later, that it's the first question of my Outer World experience.

"What the hell are you doing here?"

I shield my eyes and squint, shaking now, crying, desperate. "Jim, I can explain!"

"This is a restricted, no-access area. You can have no possible explanation," the stern voice says.

But maybe Jim will still listen to me. My courage rises. "Please, I've come all this way looking for Serenity. I must see her; I know she's alive. Please—" I try to stand but my knees feel weak, "—could you please take me to her?"

Jim pauses a second and then … laughs. "Oh, okay. Yeah, I'll be sure to do that. Let's go see Serenity now, then."

This isn't Jim? I don't think Jim would laugh, knowing that I snuck onto his ship. Also, he'd know who Serenity was, if he made a secret shipment trip five or so nights ago to get her. The light still shines in my face while a tough grip circles my upper arm. The man points the light to the ground. My eyes adjust while I'm pulled to the glass door.

"Wait. I need my bag," I tell him, leaving the blanket behind on the roof.

"I'll take your bag. I don't know what you have in there, but you've sure had enough of it."

"I'll need that," I insist.

"I hear that all the time. Whew! You reek," he says, his nose scrunched high. "Disgusting!"

"Oh," I say, deflated, my voice small. "I was sick on the ... uh ... dragonfly ship."

"The what?"

I point to the thing that brought me here.

The man shakes his head, tightening his grip. He roughly escorts me to the glass door. When we get there, he reaches for a black rectangle on his belt and gives it a squeeze.

"You mean the helicopter?"

A helicopter? I understand: the dragonfly ship is a helicopter. I nod my head but he doesn't seem to see. He is still squishing up his nose, trying to be as far from me while still grip-pinching my upper arm.

The door opens and he steers me inside, in front of a metal square. He pushes a circle button and it lights up. Magic! But I'm still thinking about how he opened the door without even touching it.

The man is using so many questions that I figure it's okay, normal even, out here.

"Where are we going?" I say, biting my lip, still blinking back tears. I study him under the light.

He's wearing a blue cap, on which is written *Riverview Security, Inc.* It covers his short brown hair and shields his eyes, so that I can't see into them. He seems younger than Dad, though I can't be sure without seeing his eyes.

The panel in front of us slides open and he pushes me in its direction. I try to jerk my arm away.

"Where are we going?" I ask, with more confidence.

"Where do you think? The Security Office," he says, as if I should know, as if, of all the dumb questions he's heard today, mine is the most ridiculous. This irks me.

"Is Serenity there?"

"Listen—" he starts again.

The panel begins to close but I lock my knees, plant my feet, and lean all my weight back, refusing to move. "Katherine," I say.

"Whatever. Okay, Katherine, listen. Here's how it goes," he says, as if he's now talking to a young child. "You were in a restricted area of the building. There are government offices in this high-rise and you are considered a threat to their security. It's after hours, see, the middle of the night, and I'm going to ask you a few questions, fill out an S-17 incident report, and then, depending on what I find in your bag, probably call the cops. Are you going to come peacefully, or am I going to use a force-hold on you? I damn well don't care what you pick, but there's just one way off this roof, and that's with me."

I try something I've never tried before: I ask a question with a question.

"Are you sending me back to the Community?"

"Gawd. Is that a brain-injury unit? If so, I'm tempted."

"You don't know about the Community? I mean, the Experiment?"

"What?" he says, rolling his eyes, his last bit of patience spent.

I get it. He doesn't know. Is this a good thing? Does that mean I'm safe?

"Okay, I'll go with you. You don't have to yank my arm off, though."

Despite the fact that this man is obnoxious and rude, I enjoy the way Outside World conversations go—so much information exchanged in a very short time. We enter the tiny room behind the panel and I see more than thirty buttons. The man pushes one of them and the door closes. Then, unexpectedly, the room drops down, fast.

My stomach lurches again. I grab my mouth to force it shut.

"Oh, gawd," he says, looking skyward. "Don't throw up on me."

I'm not sick in the elevator, but accumulated stomach acid swirls up as soon as the doors open. The man points to a circular tub just outside the hall and points, "There."

I'm busy for a while.

> *When I stop*
> *I hear you,*
> *Planet Keeper.*
> *Today you speak through a chorus of starlings*
> *Chirping in the field.*
> *Their song is always the same.*
> *But before today*
> *I could never hear you in it.*

16

Sunday, Early Morning, August 15, 2021

When I'm finished, I see the man waiting for me in a room with the door ajar, his face still all twisted up. He wordlessly points to a door and looks away.

I listen because I am embarrassed. I've never been sick in front of anybody before, except Mom, but she never made me feel as if I was vermin.

I miss Mom intensely then. I remember being sick as a child in the washing room basin and her holding back my hair and rubbing my back.

I follow the man's finger to a door. There's no doorknob, but it opens when I push it. I notice the light—not candlelight or lantern—attached to the ceiling. Inside, the room is furnished in the oddest way, so I turn around instead of going fully in.

"What is this room?"

"What kind of drugs did you take? It's called a bathroom, toilet, restroom, water closet, or ladies room. Use it to clean yourself up."

Oh, an inside outhouse. I fiddle with the gadgets on the counters. The top counter is sunk like a basin and when I try to pump for water, nothing happens. Then when I push a large button, water comes rushing out. Amazed, I wash my hands and face, then search for a drying cloth. Instead, I see the biggest looking glass I've ever seen.

I'm a mess: hair is wild, eyes are red, skin pale, almost gray. My uniform is wrinkled, and looks very odd in comparison to the man's clothing. The fabrics of his clothes seem very fine and smooth, with a tight weave and hardly any bumps or irregularities in the fabric. His jacket is a beautiful dark blue fabric—almost black—and there are shiny buttons and many pockets.

I press the top of a pump and a droplet lands in my hands. I rub my hands together and some of the black stuff comes off my skin. Still, I can't figure out where to find a hand towel.

Eventually, I return to where the man is and find him sitting at his desk. The room is sparsely decorated, very white and bright. By his desk are about fifty mini Remote screens, each showing a different view. The man watches them intently and chews on the end of a kind of pencil.

I sit down.

"Okay, I'm ready but I should really go soon. What's your first question, Brother?

"Paul. My name is Paul and I can't quite figure you out. Your bag contains no drugs or alcohol, no money, not even a bus pass."

Drugs? Alcohol? Money? Bus pass?

Brother Paul spins in his chair and dumps my bag out onto his desk. My things fall with a thud and rattle—the cheese, bread, dried fruit, matches, writing box, and knife. No one has ever disrespected my rations like this before. Domicile Inspections are never so impolite. Brother Paul's actions leave me feeling exposed, vulnerable, like when I was lying in the grass field, newly conscious, surrounded by the three shadows.

"Tell me why you were on the roof with these things."

Is everyone on the Outside World so rude?

"It might take a while, Brother Paul," I say, a chill to my voice.

"Drop the brother bit. My name is Paul—not Brother Paul, just Paul. And my shift ends in two hours," he replies. "I don't get paid for overtime, so get to it."

I look around the room, back to the elevator, wondering at my chances. Is there a way out of here without Paul?

"Don't even think about it," he says, as if reading my thoughts.

"It was in the cornfield," I begin.

"Huh?"

"I'll go back further then," I say, wondering where exactly to start.

As I finish, I notice Paul's expression has changed. Even though he's the same person, he looks different somehow, softer. We don't say anything for a minute and then he speaks.

"I think … I believe you."

"I really need to find Serenity. I promised Anna."

"She's probably at Children's Hospital of Saskatchewan."

"What's a hospital?"

"You didn't have a hospital in the Community? It's a place where sick people get referred by their doctors for specialized medical treatment."

Referred. I think about Scott, needing to be referred for his ear. "And then what?" I ask.

"The specialist doctors at the hospital improve the odds of their patients' recovery."

"Oh," I say, thinking—Children's Hospital of Saskatchewan: CHS. I gasp and get to my feet. "Can you get me there? Now?"

"I can do more than that, Katherine, though this is way out of my league. I'm just a student at the University of Saskatchewan doing security on the weekends. I'll need more evidence, but if what you are saying is true, we're talking about an unprecedented political scandal for several Prime Ministers, including our current one."

I don't follow half of his reply but I do recognize his last sentence. "I heard Father talk tonight—I mean this morning—about a Prime Minister."

"Do you have proof? And did Father's letter from the library actually mention the Prime Minister's name?"

"Not his name, but it mentioned Armed Forces. Does that help?"

"Where is it?"

"Maybe in Father's bag, but I couldn't find it in his office. Why is this important?"

"Try and understand, Katherine. The experiment is a violation of human rights. Experimentation on human life is not publicly endorsed by any government on Earth, though I'm sure they all do it."

I interrupt him. "I just want my family to be safe, to live together in a place where children with problems don't just disappear. Do you have that here?"

"Yeah, sure," Paul says, but I'm vague about what he means.

"The Outside World is like that, isn't it?" I ask him, seeking out eye contact.

But Paul is preoccupied, tapping a pen on the desk, thinking about something else. I bite my lip and look down. I just assumed the Outside World was better. Was I wrong?

"Was I right to tell you?" I wonder aloud. In my heart, I know I'm keeping my family together in the only way I know how, and keeping my promise to Anna at the same time. Even if every other factor changes for the worse, my family won't change … can't.

"I don't know what I would've done if I were you," Paul says. "All I know is your bubble existence is based on lies. There never was an Ecological Revolution, and pockets of insufficient air—that's just laughable—and if you put two people in the same room, you blow any chance of a perfect world; there can be no such thing. The closest we've come in Saskatchewan to an Ecological Revolution was when the government caused a temporary blackout … when SaskPower switched from four power sources—including coal and natural gas— to just two, wind power and hydroelectric dams."

Paul pauses here, puffs out his cheeks, and then empties them of air. "And now that I'm involved, I have to do something. I can't live with suppressed truth any more than you can."

"What do you mean?"

"We have to tell somebody, Katherine, even if it means I lose my job. This thing is big … wrong. Listen, the other guard's shift starts in fifteen minutes. I'm off in half an hour. I'll sneak you out of the building and then think of what to do next."

I nod, relieved to get away from this building's connection with Father.

I collect my things into the bag and follow Paul to the elevator, but then he keeps walking.

"If you have motion sickness so bad, we should take the stairs into the underground parking lot. We have to be careful, though. I think your 'Uncles and Aunts' work on the top floor. I've often wondered why the Community Development Offices are the most restricted in the building."

"Let's go," I urge.

Paul opens a door and we go down some stairs, hundreds of them, around and around for what he tells me is twenty-five floors. Finally, he stops and motions me to be quiet. I follow him through some halls and doors to a strange object surrounded by wheels and windows.

"What's this?"

"The company hybrid," he tells me, opening it up, and motioning me into a compartment. "Hide in the back seat."

I guess my face tells him he's lost me.

"In your world, it's a wagon," he explains, "In mine, it's called a car. Your horses eat grass for fuel; this car runs on algae bio-fuel."

I'm confused. "Your wagon eats algae? Where do you sit to hold the reins?"

Paul laughs, a bit too nervously, and shuts the compartment. I wait for him, curled up on the seat. My stomach gurgles, my head is pounding from lack of sleep, and my throat is dry and burning sore from being sick.

I'm too tired to be nervous, too exhausted to question Paul's motives for helping me. In the back of the car, I finally feel comfortable, too comfortable. I fall asleep.

The first thing I notice is that we're moving, which for me is not a good thing. I feel dizzy, but don't want to sit up. Compared to the "helicopter," this "car" sounds like a cat purring.

"Paul?"

"Put your seat belt on, Katherine," he tells me. "We've cleared the parkade security, so we're good."

I sit up and look around. Paul's world spins by and my eyes find it impossible to focus. Dawn is breaking in this strange place and the orange-peach glow of the morning sun shines off the windows of giant buildings. It's overwhelming and I cry out, covering my eyes.

Paul slows the car a few minutes later and helps me. Reaching for my hand, he clicks what he calls the seat belt. Then he tucks my bag next to me.

"Want a mint?" he asks me.

"Like a herb sprig? You chew on them here, too?"

"I just thought you might need one," he says, passing me a small, round white ball. "It's a candy."

I put it in my mouth, but then spit it out and hide it in my hand. It's sickeningly sweet. "Thank you," I say to Paul. "Please, do you have any water?" I ask him. "Is there a pump nearby? I'm so thirsty."

Paul goes back to his seat. "No, we'll have to stop for some drinks. Wait. You'll love this. I'll show you something that will blow your grid."

I just nod my head as Paul presses a button and makes the car move again.

Some people pass Paul's car, dressed in strange, colorful clothes. Cars are everywhere, traveling in different directions; wires hang from poles above the ground, and buildings far and wide block the skyline. Paul's world is too busy. Objects are on the ground, in the air, beside the car—all shapes, sizes, and colors. There is even a tiny Remote screen next to Paul with figures and details.

I feel nauseous just looking out the windows and wish I had some blinders, like the ones Brother Joel puts on the newly trained horses. I rest my head against the back of the seat and close my eyes. I think about life on the farm, of Mom and Dad, who are just waking up, and Scott—who will soon be sent to wake me. My stomach tightens.

"So, this isn't your car?" I ask Paul, in an attempt to think of something else.

"This? No, not mine. I'm more of a transit person myself," he says, with a forced chuckle. "But taking the bus with you would be disastrous. My boss won't mind if I borrow this for the day—I hope. It belongs to Riverview, the company I work for," Paul says. He stops to bite a nail. "I could get fired for taking it out; it's supposed to be for emergencies. Get it?"

I shake my head.

"When there's a security threat in this city, then whoever is on duty locks down the building and drives to help secure the other Riverview buildings. It only happens about once a year with supply problems, but we have to be prepared, just in case. Usually things are pretty low-key around here, though."

My head is still pounding and the movement of the car makes me feel dizzy. I imagine pumping water into a bucket and of how refreshing it would be to dunk my head. I feel us slowing down. I look up through the front glass. Paul is driving to the side of a yellow and red building.

"Why are we stopping?" I ask him.

"Breakfast," he says. "My treat." Then Paul laughs again. "Well, you know, because you don't know how to use money."

I don't say anything. I just watch him as he pulls up to a box next to a busy sign full of food pictures, writing, and numbers. The box starts speaking, loud mumbles I can't quite understand, but Paul knows what to do.

"Yeah, we'll get a number three combo and a number one." Paul turns to me then, with a big smile and says, "You're going to love this part of our world." Then, back to the box he says, "And a number five, too, but with two orange juices, and an ice water."

Paul pulls the car ahead, closer to the building then, and I watch, incredulous, as an older woman smiles at Paul, takes some paper from him; she hands him two brown bags and a brown tray with cups on it. Then she puts something small and jingly into his palm. Paul tells me that it's called "change."

The car is filled with a strong aroma, something I can't name, but it hangs heavy in the air. Paul is happy now, obviously hungry, but cheerful to share with me. "Try this," he tells me, holding out something wrapped in yellow paper, something that looks like egg between buns. The smell turns my stomach.

"Looks good," I lie, putting it on the seat next to me.

"Eat up," he tells me, his mouth full of egg. "I got us lots of food."

"Thanks," I say, trying not to be ungrateful. "Could I please have some water?"

"Yeah, sure," Paul says, turning around and handing me something orange. "But try this first."

"How do I open it?" I ask, looking at the cold, opaque cylinder with a shiny lid.

"Just peel back the foil," Paul tells me.

I take the "foil" and pull it back slightly, revealing a kind of juice. I take a big sip, and the super-sweet drink refreshes my mouth but then burns down my raw throat.

"Oh," I say, biting my lip to keep from crying.

"Oranges rock, eh? Did you have oranges in the Community?"

"No," I say. "Do they grow on a vine or a tree?"

"A tree, I think," Paul tells me. "Not hungry?" he asks.

"Just thirsty," I admit, returning the egg thing.

"Here's your water," he says, passing me the "water."

I take the strange cup with a pencil object poking through the top of the lid. "What is this?"

"You mean the straw?"

I nod. Straw? As in bedding for the horses?

"You suck on it and the water comes up."

After a few failed attempts resulting in bubbles, I meet with success and the water slides into my mouth, cold as winter water from our pump. It soothes and refreshes my parched, sore mouth and I sigh in happy relief, my drink rattling as I rest it on my knee. I peel off the top to discover why the water is so noisy.

"There's ice in here," I tell Paul. "This is so special. Thank you. Can I keep the cup? And maybe the straw, if you don't need it?"

"No, we'll throw it out. Pass your garbage up when you're done. I don't want to mess up my boss's car."

"But why would you throw out something so valuable? And where would you put it? And what happens then?"

The car slows down, and Paul mutters under his breath, "Traffic."

"What's that?" I ask, but he doesn't answer.

"Oh, for gawd's sake." He turns onto a smaller road, houses on both sides of us. I see tiny garden plots and large sheds, probably the outhouses, and each yard is surrounded by its own type of fence.

"Let's take the highway," Paul says, more to himself. We speed ahead, much faster now, my stomach whiffling like a yearling goose. "We're just entering the University gates."

"Oh," I say, looking out the window, but I don't see a scenery difference. The buildings look just as packed together; the cars zip past and around us at alarming speeds. Paul is calm, though, not concerned. I close my eyes again to block out his hectic world, trying to let the water smother my volcanic stomach.

"Who is gawd?" I ask Paul, watching him again.

"What?" he says, reaching into his jacket pocket.

"Gawd. You said, 'For gawd's sake.'"

"Oh," Paul laughs. "I'm sure I don't know." He pulls out a black rectangle from his jacket and pushes a few buttons on it.

"Then why say it?"

"Everyone does. Gawd is, you know, the big boss."

"You mean the Planet Keeper?"

"Planet Keeper? Yeah, I guess so. Don't think about it much." Paul holds the black rectangle to his ear. "Hello?"

Is he talking to me?

"Too early?" He listens a second, then says, "Hey, can I come over? I have something for you. Five minutes. Bye, Asha." Paul presses a button, and then puts the thing down.

"Who's Asha?"

Paul meets my gaze through a looking glass attached to the front window.

"I've figured out what we're going to do, Katherine. My friend, Asha, is a Communications student, preparing for a career in the Media. She'll know how to help us."

"Media?" As in what Father showed Dad?

"Yeah, this." Paul pushes a button near the mini-Remote and a female voice interrupts him. "In other news, two ..."

"Who said that?" I scream.

Paul winces and grabs his ears, touching the button again. "Gawd, Katherine. Relax. It's just an audio-communication network channel."

"What?"

"Like a radio, only three-dimensional. Asha can explain how it works."

"Three dimensional?" I shake my head. Is a radio similar to the Remote?

Paul's eyes meet mine. "Don't let technology scare you."

How can fifty thousand new things not intimidate me?

"It's just a voice signal bounced off a satellite that our car can pick up and split into layers. I'm going to try again. This is my favorite news anchor, Marina Era, and she always covers political stories that the other stations don't touch."

"In related news, residents in the area are advised to be on the lookout for a fifteen-year-old female runaway who suffers from severe dementia due to head-trauma. She is known to the RCMP simply as *Katherine* and should be considered a dangerous threat to security. For a picture of this fugitive, press the number sign on your monitor."

I open my eyes. Is that woman talking about me?

Paul presses the button on the screen and there I am—a picture of me with my short hair—on the Remote in our car!

Something is wrong. Something is horribly wrong!

"Oh, gawd! Katherine, get down, get down! Gawd! I'm gonna lose my job, get kicked out of school. Just take off the seat belt and sit on the floor."

"What's happening, Paul?" I ask, struggling with the belt. How does this thing release? And why does Paul keep yelling for gawd every time he's angry or scared? Is gawd someone who helps him, as the Planet Keeper does for me?

I knock the water; the ice stays behind while the water seeps through the seat.

"We have to get to Asha's. Cover yourself with your jacket and, whatever you do, stay down."

"I can't release the seat belt," I say, tears brimming my eyes.

"Lie on the seat anyway," he tells me. "Now!"

I do and the belt cuts into my waist. I can trust Paul, right?

Paul cracks his knuckles while he drives, and twitches every time he says the car has to stop for a "red light."

"Will the media help us, Paul?"

"It's the only way now, Katherine. If I bring you to the RCMP or Canadian Security Intelligence Service, you'll be back in the Community, digging out potatoes."

"That's likely the Role I'd get anyway," I tell Paul.

Paul pauses and takes a moment to think. Then he shakes his head. "Crop harvests are all done by machines and computers now."

Farming by machine? What would Dad think?

Mom & Dad:
All I want
Is for you to look at me
And be proud of what you see.
But
I have to be someone
I'm proud of, too.

17

Sunday, August 15, 2021

Asha's building isn't as big as the one Paul works in. He parks in something like a dim cave below the structure and turns off the sound of the car.

"Listen, Katherine. I have to prepare Asha for this and make sure the coast is clear. I'll be back in ten minutes."

Coast? Paul is gone for what feels like almost an hour. The whole time he's away, I'm as nervous as a goose on a nest with a river otter nearby. What if Paul and Asha are contacting Father right now? Should I leave and go on my own to find Serenity? How far can I get in this world without money, or a car, with the RCMP—whoever they are—after me?

I look out the windows and chew my lip. Serenity needs a hospital. I may be able to find her at CHS, but I won't be able to take her home, not by walking, not by sneaking onto a helicopter at the end of the month. How will I reunite Anna and Serenity? How will I see my family again?

I think about the Community, about Dad. I was naïve to think I was the only one in the Community with questions. Over the years, people at home have made a choice and chosen the Community, picking security over the truth. If I had known the real choice was between my family and these answers, I would never have gotten onto the helicopter. But is it too late to have both?

Finally, I see Paul running to the car. He sits in the front seat and whispers to me without turning around. Why is Paul acting so strange?

"Asha is upstairs in her dormitory room. Don't worry." He reaches under his coat. "Here, put these on. They'll fit you." Paul hands me a long, thin, blue jacket and a hat of some kind.

"What am I supposed to do?"

"Your clothes give you away, so hurry—put those on. Asha thinks we're lucky if they haven't already traced the missing hybrid."

"Who are 'they'?" I ask, looking down. My clothes look like dirty, rough, brown burlap bags compared to the fabrics of Paul's world.

"My boss, the RCMP, your Community Development people. I'm assuming Father is the one who contacted the RCMP to look for you. He'll know you could only get as far as the roof without some kind of help. I was the one monitoring your sector last night, so it's natural my boss will assume I can give the RCMP what they want: you."

I put the hat on and then the jacket. "Okay," I say, drawing a deep breath. "Let's go."

Asha is not one for light conversation. As soon as Paul and I reach her room, she locks the door and shuts the white drapes. She's a tiny mouse of a woman with hair even shorter than Paul's or mine. She has the widest eyes I've ever seen, sparkles on her eyelids, long, thick black lashes, big red lips, and metal things hanging from her ear lobes. I stare at them while she talks. She also isn't one for clothes. I try not to look, but I can see her bare arms, her neck down to her breastbone, and she is wearing a skirt that doesn't reach to her knees. And her feet are astonishing. She has on strange black, shiny shoes, and the backs of them are arched high, as if she is standing on part of a knitting needle.

"I need to know more of what we're dealing with, Katherine. Paul summarized things but I need details, five minutes' worth."

I sense her tension and spill information quickly, until I feel like I'm the babbling brook back home.

She nods her head in small jerky movements, at the same time reaching for a small silver box from which she pulls out a white thing the size of a small pencil. She creates fire from a tiny metal cylinder, puts the flame to the white paper thing in her mouth, and then draws in a deep breath, making the end of the pencil thing burn orange, then cinder black. She exhales the smoke into my face and I start to cough.

"I get the picture. Hang for a second."

Hang? I cough and more smoke burns my eyes. I stagger away from the pair, looking for a window while trying to navigate Asha's room of dark furniture. I reach the drapes and feel my way to fresh air.

"Don't touch the window," Asha orders, and then turns back to Paul.

"Are you thinking what I am?"

"If we arrange a meeting in person with someone—"

"We'd be surrounded in minutes."

"Right. I bet the RCMP and CSIS have all the frequencies monitored."

"Especially if they've traced me to you."

Despite the tension, I'm amused by the way they finish each other's sentences, as if they're sharing one brain and neither has to guess anything because they are so direct.

"Who knows we're together? Anyone at your work? School friends? Your mom?"

"They've contacted her, I imagine," Paul says.

"Definitely," Asha nods, breathing smoke over Paul's head. "Let's assume our cell phone lines are monitored … and you called me over an hour ago."

"Then we may have minutes before we're arrested. Asha, I'm sorry."

"Are you kidding, Paul? We haven't done anything wrong and we don't have anything to lose." Asha scans the room, snuffs out her smoky thing into a dish, and grabs two black bags.

I guess Asha packed while I was in the car downstairs. She motions for us to be quiet and to follow her.

What's going on?

Asha enters the hall and twists a button on her door. We go down the stairs a few "floors" and enter another room. This one is even tinier than Asha's but it is much more interesting; plants and cats are everywhere.

"We're safe here while we make a plan," she tells us, moving to check windows and close the drapes. "Tammy is at work. We're key-buddies, so in case she has to work late, I feed her cats."

"Does anyone know you're friends?" Paul asks her.

"Well, you didn't," Asha says. "So that's something, at least. I met Tammy in the laundry room."

"Can I borrow the outhouse?" I interrupt them with some urgency.

Asha looks at me, incredulous. "You can't be serious."

I squeeze my legs together and fidget, wondering what she'll do if I wet myself on her friend's carpet.

Asha strides over to a door near me. "Here," she says, exhaling loudly. "Can you figure out how to use this? You pee into the water, and then push the silver button to flush it away."

She exits and I hastily attend to my business. Later, while marveling at the lights, vials, taps, paper, and gadgets, a knock at the door brings me back to focus.

"You fall in?" Asha calls, then laughs.

I open the door. Before I leave, I take a dollop of some delicious-smelling strawberry hand salve and rub my hands.

"Are you ready?" Paul asks Asha.

"I just need to write down this number," she tells him, looking at a black device she holds in her hand. "Then we'll phone Marina Era from the square ... which gives her less time to brush us off."

Her? Phone?

"Are you happy?" I ask them, eyeing the room. "I mean, what's it like, living without wide, open spaces and places to enjoy the outdoors, the birds?"

Asha gives Paul a look and he turns around.

"Uh ... listen, Katherine. No offense, but we're in a time crunch here. We can only help you ... if you're quiet."

A black cat rubs against my shin. I distract myself by playing with her and the other cats. After a while, I get agitated. I can't remember the last time I only cared about food, water, and play. So, is the Outer World better?

"Think this will work?" I hear Asha say to Paul.

"You're the Communications student. Your degree has to be worth something."

"Okay, so then I'll take the keys, and bring Tammy's car to the garage stairwell. You follow in five with Katherine, right?"

Paul kisses Asha good-bye, and I look away. Are we doing the right thing?

Ten minutes later, we're in Tammy's car. Asha and Paul are in the front seat, and I'm in the back again, squatting on the floor.

"Where are we going?" I ask them.

"Don't worry, just stay down," Paul tells me.

I do, except after about twenty minutes, my legs cramp in this small space. I stretch and move so I'm lying on the seat, my eyes on the ceiling of the car. When I tilt my head back and look out the top of the windows, I see a different view, as if I'm looking at the Outside World from upside down. And if my jacket had covered me then, and we weren't stopped at a "red light," I would've missed the sign: CHS.

"Oh!" I say, sitting up, excited.

"Lie down!" Asha yells. "What are you doing?"

"I have to go," I say, reaching for the door handle, and pulling it out as I saw Paul do. I exit the car and am surrounded on all sides by other cars, all lined up for the light. A few of these honk at me, like angry geese, and I pull Asha's blue cap over my ears, then run for a tree. Asha yells, "Come back—now!"

The light changes then, and the cars start moving again. Even Tammy's car is forced forward by incessant, blaring horns.

From behind the tree and across the street, I see the Children's Hospital of Saskatchewan and, when there's a break in traffic, I run for it, just as Paul and Asha manage to turn the car around farther on up the road.

Running up the path to the hospital, I arrive at the doors, out of breath, my nerves both tingly and excited.

Serenity! I kept my promise, Anna!

The large glass doors baffle me a moment, and I try to figure them out. A woman approaches from the other side and the doors slide open for her, no touch necessary. I enter and survey the entrance area for any clue that might help me. There are "elevators" and different "floors" with terms and names I've never heard of. I walk over to the Information Desk, and wait to speak to a woman wearing a type of blue uniform.

"I'm looking for someone," I tell her.

"Name?"

"Katherine."

"What's her last name?"

"No, that's my name. I'm looking for Serenity."

The woman takes a deep breath. "Last name?"

"I … don't know," I say, unsure of what she is asking. My eyes fill up.

"Then I can't help you," the woman says, forcing a smile. "The system doesn't register given names, and we don't give out personal information about our patients to their friends unless they give us both the first *and* last names."

The man behind me clears his throat and the woman turns to him, her eyes off me.

"Wait!" I tell her. "Serenity is six years old with dark skin and black hair—in patches—I think, under a wig. She came here early Monday morning ... almost a week ago. Please ... please ... I have to see her. Her sister ... sent me," I say, my eyes brimming tears.

"This is a big hospital," the woman tells me, gently. "And I can't help you without your friend's last name. Sorry, honey."

What do I do now? Serenity could be anywhere in this building. I might never find her, and even if I searched around, she could be locked up behind another fixed door with someone blocking her from leaving.

But I have to try. I hurry to the "elevators."

"That's not the way to find her," the woman says, calling after me.

I press the button and it lights up. I look back at the woman. She is holding a device to her ear and staring at me.

The elevator opens and I dash in. The door closes as I see the woman jogging towards me.

"Stop!" she says, holding her hand out.

Inside, I press the first button I see. The elevator goes up a few seconds and opens on a floor with the word *Cardiology*.

I dart out into the hall and see a sign with the hospital map. My eyes skim the words—so many I don't know—for a clue. *Neonatal, Renal Dialysis, CT Scan, MRI, Radiology, Ambulatory Care, Hematology, Oncology, Laboratory* ... but where is Serenity?

I start walking down one hall ... and then another. It seems everywhere I go, people look at me, stop me, question me.

"Are you lost?" a man asks.

"No," I say, walking away.

Around a corner, a woman says, "Excuse me?"

"You're excused," I tell her, with my most polite smile, then keep searching.

"You can't go in there," another tells me when I get to the last door of the "floor."

Walking to a window, I look out and see a beautiful flower garden—arranged with all kinds of strange and wonderful colors of flowers I've never seen—next to a water fountain, some benches nearby.

I find my way out there and sit, my head in my hands, weeping. What do I do now, Planet Keeper? And that's where Paul and Asha find me, both exhaling angry words about gawd and something called hell.

"Don't you ever just need quiet?" I ask them, taking a deep breath and looking up to the sky. "That's what I miss: three hundred and sixty degrees of silence, of birds, and wind, and the sound of sunlight as it touches a wheat stalk. You don't have that here."

"Why don't you show it to us now, then?" Asha says, her arms folded on her chest.

Paul goes over to her, whispers something into her neck and she walks away, reaching into a small black bag and lighting up one of the smoky, white pencil things.

"She stinks," I tell Paul, and he waves her farther away.

I take another deep breath, closing my eyes to concentrate. A low vibration comes from near the hospital; beyond that, cars. But almost a minute later, I find the sound I want: birds, in a bush. Chickadees?

"What are you doing?" Paul asks, now less impatient.

"Serenity is in there," I tell him. "She was referred, but I don't know where she is, what her last name is."

"Father would have some kind of security on her floor; no doubt she'd be locked up. There's just no way to get to her. And if the hospital security hasn't seen your picture on the news yet, they will soon. Then they'll recognize you sitting out here."

Paul turns his head and looks around. "I see two cameras pointing at us right now. What was your plan when you got here?"

"Oh," I say, starting to cry. "I didn't imagine it like this. I thought going out *through the sky* would be a help for my family and that I'd find something good."

"Hey, how could you know?" Paul says, with a fake laugh, lightly patting me on the back. "Security will be here, soon. Let's go."

I move my shoulders in the opposite direction and Paul gets the message to drop his arm.

I look over at Asha, whose eyes implore us to move off the bench and back into the car.

"We live in very different worlds," I tell Paul. "And in many ways, my Community is better. You don't cook your own food, or know life without motion. You have so many things that you've lost an ability to be content with simplicity. Are you even happy?"

"What?" But Paul doesn't answer me. Then he says, "You don't have to live in a city, Katherine. You have choices now."

Choices. I think about that a minute.

"You've never had a real choice, but here's your first one. The RCMP and CSIS are looking for you. And when they find you, they will lock you up to keep you quiet and take away your future. Your time is running out … and you can't survive here without us. You have zero street smarts and you look like an alien."

Paul takes a deep breath. "So what would you think of taking us to your community instead? Asha and I think it's the only way. If we get there before the RCMP get you, they wouldn't dare take away your freedom, not when the whole world is watching."

"The whole world? Beyond the City?"

"You've never had a real choice, Katherine, but you certainly don't have one now. Sometimes choice is an illusion," Paul tells me, pulling me to my feet.

"Maybe freedom is, too," I say, following him back to the car.

Asha is a bit nicer after that. Later, in the helicopter, I sit next to three men I don't know, in a row behind Marina Era, Asha, and Paul.

I'm not sick the second time I fly. I'm sure it's because I have nothing in my stomach except a pill my seatmate gave me for motion sickness.

I overhear Paul and Asha narrate my story while Marina takes notes. Often I try to interject, or contradict them outright. Sometimes they listen, but mostly they talk as if I can't understand their language.

"What do think of the title *Lone Roof Girl*, for my book?" Paul asks Asha. "I should take notes now, maybe sketch an outline. Just think, I'll be the first writer in that community, the first to collect unspoiled firsthand research."

How could Paul write my story if he doesn't know my life?

Asha replies, "She's going to be an immigrant in the country of her birth. That would be a good title if you could somehow shorten it. Think of it: life with no birth certificate, or passport, no useful education, no knowledge of technology, clueless on fashion, or shopping, or money. Gawd, it sucks to be her."

I sit there, my mouth open, words slow to my tongue.

Marina interjects then, looking over her shoulder at me, a flicker of kindness there. "Yes, but she has also had a beautiful, organic, healthy upbringing without deadlines, ownership, materialism, waste, religion, homelessness, poverty, or crime. It was almost idyllic."

"Almost," Asha says, "if brown is your color."

Marina touches my hand. "The government will retrain you—of course—and provide an apology in time. There will be financial assistance, and those who stay behind in the Community will probably get to keep their land as a kind of settlement—but no more funding. Katherine, you might even be able to pay for college by doing a few talk shows. Would you enjoy that?"

I bite my lip, looking away.

One of her devices rings then, and she puts it to her ear. She listens for a bit, then snaps it shut. To Paul and Asha she says, "Looks like the Community Development Offices were funded via the Canadian Armed Forces budget. And the Aunts and Uncles were actually soldiers, now rich soldiers, promised pensions if they kept their mouths shut."

Asha laughs. "This story keeps getting bigger. Are you still up for your promise? One of your cameramen will follow me around the Community with a microphone after we land?"

"Yes, yes," says Marina, brushing out her hair. "You'll get your career in front of a camera. That was the deal." Her device rings again, and she announces, "The Prime Minister is going to make a statement on our network and respond to allegations that he plans to change parties in the next election—to the Ecological Socialists. Everyone at the Network gets early bonuses."

It takes them about four hours, and a refueling stop, to find the Experiment, using their gadgets and devices. I guess the Community, which I'm told exists in a no-fly zone, is difficult to find unless you know where to look on an Armed Forces map. Eventually, I become hungry for my bread and cheese. I offer some to Paul, but he prefers his food—flat bars of some kind wrapped in shiny paper. It's too bad for him; he would've loved my Mom's bread, even if it *is* a day old.

It's about four in the afternoon when we approach the Community. As I look down, I realize why everything had to be beige and browns. The Community is hidden in this setting, even in daylight, and as beautiful as a Canada goose in cattails and wild grass. A quote from the Manifesto pops into my head as we approach the Residential Areas: *It is better to fit into your natural surroundings than to stand out.*

Marina tells the pilots to land in the Town Center. As the helicopter begins to descend, I feel queasy, not just from the air travel, but as if I am standing between two worlds, neither of them my home. Dread fills my limbs and I clasp my hands to keep them from shaking.

I tell myself that Serenity will be reunited with her family and Scott won't disappear now, not ever. Still, my courage seeps away and tears dam up behind my eyes.

Marina and her crew rush out of the helicopter and "roll the tape live" just seconds after we touch land. Asha jumps in front of a "camera" and tells the man holding it to focus back on me. She speaks into a black stick device while I fumble with the seatbelt.

"Hello. My name is Asha Vines, reporting from Canada's own Community Experiment. I'm here with Katherine, who is returning to her people after exposing their secret existence to the world. Katherine. What are your thoughts right now?"

I cover my head with my jacket and reach for the opposite door of the helicopter, slamming it behind me.

Across the Circle, I see Community members looking out from behind drapes in their windows or hiding in the lanes. A few brave ones approach the helicopter—Eric's father, Brother Roy, Brother Michael, and Brother Thad, the butcher.

I watch their faces as the wall of lies tumbles down. I see their thoughts—shock, confusion, anger, doubt, and grief. They look at me and I look away, my face hot. I have let the bear into their home and it will destroy everything in its wide-angle view.

The helicopter "engine" shuts off and a gathering group of Community members approaches. Marina and Asha try to talk to them but the people snub all their questions, as they have been trained so well to do.

I search the growing crowd for my parents, for Anna.

Another helicopter approaches and I hear his voice, even in all the noise.

"You're home safe. I'm so … relieved," Father says, his arms outstretched for me. "You had us quite worried."

I feel his hug, my hands by my side, my body stiff.

"I'm not angry," he says. "I love you. You were curious. Curiosity can be okay, I think. Come now, let's get away from the cameras and talk this out."

Asha nudges a "camera" man and they watch us.

I turn and step away.

Father follows me. "You've seen the outside so you know both worlds. I think it will make a powerful statement to the country, to our people, when you choose this life and stay here. You have wisdom and perspective now. Those are essential qualities in a young Community Leader."

I hardly hear him. I stand on tiptoe, tears now falling, looking for Dad's head above the others.

"Father, what is happening?" Sister Ann implores him.

"I don't understand," someone murmurs.

I walk amongst the crowd. Some reach for me, some touch my arms, but I look over them, around them. Where is my family?

Father is following me, with Asha behind him.

He says, "The Socialist party is growing in Canada. They need us to succeed since this Community is their prototype. They believe Canada's hope for survival lies in replicating small communities like these. Would you prefer a Role in their new government?"

I ignore him, searching in all directions, skimming over faces— the angry ones, the lost ones, the crying ones.

But Father keeps talking to me.

"You could write, you know, and not just stories. We need a more elaborate Manifesto for the country and educational curriculum for schools. Is that something you'd enjoy overseeing?"

Father touches my shoulder and I meet his eyes. They brim with something I don't recognize in him … panic?

He frowns, pulling at his forehead. "You know, I only really deceived you about one thing. The Ecological Revolution hasn't happened ... but it will ... and soon. Here our people will be safe. I pity our race, what they will endure, but we can survive and outlast any storm that the planet throws our way as it reacts to Global Warming."

"Oh!" I cry, thinking of the City. "How horrible for all those people."

A sad smile spreads on Father's face and he reaches for me again.

"Welcome home," he says. "I'm glad you're back where you should be."

Then Father looks at Asha, not me, a look of triumph in his eyes.

It's only a split second, but I know then that Father doesn't care about people at all, and my courage grows. I pull away from him.

"No," I say, jumping back.

Father gasps and looks as if he might cry.

"No ... to everything," I tell him, shaking my head.

Father's eyes flash a moment—instant anger—and he takes a step forward.

We start a dangerous game then, always moving, always five leap-strides apart, dodging people, weaving in and out of the crowds and cameras so that I can't be caught.

"Who is going to help you find a new home?" he asks, his teeth clenched into a smile, one cheek twitching. "Your new friends in the media? They'll be out of your life in two days. Then where will you be?"

"With my family," I shout, surprising even myself. From my peripheral vision, I scan the crowd for my parents, but they aren't anywhere.

"You can be with them here," Father says. "Scott can have his little operation."

I dodge more people to increase my distance from Father.

"You don't know what you're doing," Father says. "Stop and listen to reason. It's a wild world out there. This is the safest place for Scott."

I'm too stirred to respond, but he's right. I don't know the implications—can't possibly know them all. Was I wrong? Should I never have climbed aboard that helicopter and, instead, let Dad negotiate for Scott's safety?

Father's face is red now, and his voice wavers. "What is it you want? Do you want to help the world? Do you want to make a difference? This whole project has been about creating the conditions for future generations to experience perfection."

I shake my head. "But we didn't have perfection. You made Serenity disappear."

"She's alive because she's receiving treatment for cancer."

"But scared and alone … separated from her family. You made Mom lose all those babies," I sputter.

"For science's sake; all in the name of future hope. How could a child understand this?" Father's face freezes into a thin smile.

"You would've destroyed Mom if you took Scott." An image fills my mind. I remember crouching behind the planter, defeated … and I don't want to feel like that again.

I stand my ground, fists extended.

Father stops, too, wipes at his eyes and says, "Our hope is in learning to control imperfections; increasing control of our lives."

"No," I say, "as long as one person has control, there is no hope for the others."

Sister Margaret finds Father then, gasping for breath, her cheeks flushed.

"You have to get this situation under control," she tells him, in a loud, frantic whisper. "Everyone is asking for you."

Father points at Asha and the camera man.

"It would be a great help to me if you could show those people our school," Father tells Sister Margaret. "They need to see the Community's features and accomplishments beyond the Town Circle. There is no one else I would trust with this important task."

Sister Margaret's face brightens into a proud smile. "Of course," she says, with a quick glance at me before she looks back at Father. "I won't disappoint you."

Then Sister Margaret steps forward to engage Asha in conversation.

From the corner of my eye, I see Dad running past the Main Community Building into the Town Circle.

If I can just get away from Father.

I turn from him, pushing past a few people. Two steps more … and I am pulled back into the lane. Father circles my waist and arms to restrain me. I try to break free but his grip around my diaphragm winds me and I am lost for breath.

"Dad!" I call out, just before Father covers my mouth with his hand. I ignore the dull throb in my forehead and try to bite at his palm.

"Why couldn't you be like the others?" he moans into my ear. I kick my legs backwards, as a donkey would, until I connect—hard—with Father's shin. He collapses and lets me go.

"I am like my dad and that's enough," I yell, running past Asha, finally free.

Dad is by the helicopter, wildly looking through the crowd, my purple book in one hand. Anna told him about it.

I run into his arms and he holds me until my tears stop.

He sobs into my boy hair. "I'm sorry. I knew about the airplane. I wrote the note for the other dissident farmers. You said in your letter that you were sorry we couldn't talk. I was afraid I'd never have a chance to fix that."

Someone touches my arm and I look behind me: Anna.

"I know where Serenity is," I say, holding Anna by the shoulders, my voice breaking. "Go get your family and you'll be with her again before nightfall."

Anna looks at me, at first incredulous, and then her lips quiver into a smile. She turns and darts back into the crowd.

Mom runs when she spots us, and Scott, too.

We embrace and Scott grips my waist in a tight hug.

Mom is crying. Is she angry?

I watch her, unsure of what to say, of how to talk to her. Scott is quiet. He holds one of my hands with all ten of his little fingers.

Dad says, "I should've been the one to take us all out."

Mom interrupts him. "No, I wouldn't let you. I was terrified, afraid we'd lose everything. I held you to an old deal." Tears pour down her face as she looks at me. "I thought you were lost. I'm so … happy."

"What was the deal?" I ask.

Mom hesitates, so Dad answers my question. "When you were born, after our long journey to have a child, I promised you—and your Mom—that I would always keep you safe, always work to provide the best life possible for you. For years, we tried to convince ourselves that meant ignoring the problems around us."

Dad puts an arm around Mom and gazes down at my purple book. Then he looks up and motions for us to load onto a helicopter. I turn and see that Anna's family is loading onto one next to ours.

"We request asylum in Canada," Dad tells the pilot.

"How do you know those words?" I ask him.

"I can learn from a dictionary, too," Dad says, sitting down next to me.

I grin and show him how to use a seat belt.

Scott leans his head onto my arm. "Why did you have to go?"

I look to my parents, take a deep breath, and smile. "Where do we begin?"

The wind blows the grass
In all directions.
Like a multitude of people
All talking at once.
So much to say
And then
Silence.

Interview with P.J. Sarah Collins

It's always interesting to know what inspires a writer to tell a certain story. What triggered your interest in Katherine's situation in this novel?

Katherine is a courageous young woman in pursuit of truth, willing to risk everything to find it … and just thinking about a person like that made me wonder about myself. Is it possible to be an independent thinker if I am constantly digesting information and disinformation … and am never alone with my own thoughts? Though the Remote in Katherine's world is on for less than an hour a day and functions as a news program with some simple entertainment content, Father is able to manipulate his captive audience for a medical scan. I wonder in what ways I am being manipulated through media in my world. As a citizen, do I have access to the full story of my community, my country? These questions triggered a story idea which led to more questions.

Father wishes to be seen as a benign leader. Why do you think he felt it would be wise to leave his Community ignorant of their origins, rather than telling them about his rationale for setting up this isolated society?

In previous drafts, I wrote Father as dictatorial and detached, the stereotype of top-down authoritarian leadership. In reality, it read as inauthentic because Father deeply loves his Community and wrestles with how much truth his people need to live good lives. He selectively chooses information for them, as a parent would, as our politicians and leaders do for us, too. I think Father concluded that political ideologies, world religions, and higher levels of math and literature, for example, were all unnecessary for his purpose, his experiment. Without religion, what is the point of telling people of their origins? Origins remind people of their diversity and Father wanted his people to unite for the tasks ahead, to embrace *now*. To do this, I think he had to convince them that the real issues they faced were survival vs. extinction.

Throughout the narrative, Katherine is always asking questions—of herself and others. How important is the asking of questions in developing human intelligence?

But what are questions but the seeking of truth or the probing of a mystery? Do questions build IQ in people? Are inquisitive people more intelligent? Helen Keller couldn't ask questions of her world until she had a language ... but she had a high IQ. Now I'm curious. I'll have to ask a social scientist. However, I suspect that life's grandest questions and mysteries cannot be answered in science. Often our biggest questions linger, unanswered. Maybe it takes a lifetime to formulate the starting questions: Why are we alive in this time and place? Why is anything here, instead of nothing?

Do you think there are virtues to the way of life practiced by members of the Community? What are they?

Marina Era sums up some of the Community's virtues when she tells Asha that Katherine, "had a beautiful, organic, healthy upbringing without deadlines, ownership, materialism, waste, religion, homelessness, poverty, or crime. It was almost idyllic." The Community is a group of people from multi-ethnic backgrounds, sharing things in common, where all have a Role and rations for what they need—food, clothing, homes. It sounds like a nice place to visit—clean, quaint, quiet, and well-ordered.

Their mode of conversing requires patience and politeness. They rely on each other for survival and exist a sustainable, pollution-free way. I find some aspects of their education intriguing, too, in providing knowledge about the environment and survival skills. Prenursing, for example, helps Katherine take care of her own burn, and I like that the school helps meet Community needs. I think the students feel they are important contributors to their society (beyond the child-labor implications).

In history and in fiction, there are other examples of societies that have been sealed off from the rest of the world, in hopes of achieving a degree of perfection not known to most of us. Are there any of these examples that particularly inspired you?

When my husband and I traveled around Northern Ireland and Ireland, we often sought accommodation where it was available—bed and breakfasts, monasteries, and abbeys. We met a lovely Benedictine monk who corresponded with us for years and we loved learning about how his order lived. Later, when we moved to Northern Ireland for two years, we worked for nine months in a Reconciliation Community. As the country struggled with the peace process, we lived with Catholics and Protestants, Europeans, and North Americans under the same roof. We shared resources, living spaces, duties, and stories. Living like this was counter-intuitive and humbling, but was a wonderful experience for us as new immigrants, learning our way around a fascinating new culture. (I rewrote this book while living in County Down, including scenes like the library where Katherine found Father's letter and Sister Millie cut her hair.)

Community is an ongoing theme that intrigues me. One could argue that history is really just a collection of communities trying to find a sustainable way to live—or exploding and reshaping until they can figure it out.

When Katherine escapes from the Community, she finds that the outside world isn't perfect, either. What are you saying about the pursuit for perfection that idealists often focus on?

While some idealists think that the bad things of life can be systematically removed, or that human nature is generally good if ambition and selfishness can be brought under control, I agree with Paul when he tells Katherine, "If you put two people in the same room, you blow any chance of a perfect world."

I like what one English author wrote when invited by *The Times* in 1908 to respond to the question: *What is Wrong with the World?*

Dear Sirs, I am. Sincerely yours, G.K. Chesterton.

As humans we keep trying to create ideal governments, institutions, neighborhoods, or even marriages … but we seem to be incapable of doing this because the ultimate problem is an internal me first glitch inside us, not something external to our environment.

Though you have already had one other book published, you are still in the early stages of your writing career. What advice do you have for young writers?

Find other writers. Eight years before my first book was released, I was invited to join a writers' group led by Alison Acheson. In this way, over fourteen years and different projects, I have been able to shadow my favorite author, be encouraged and challenged by other writers, and keep learning what I *must* do … to process life, through metaphor and story.

PJ Sarah Collins is a children's novelist and teacher in Vancouver where she lives with her husband and three children. She is author of *Sam and Nate*, a junior novel. For more on PJ Sarah Collins please go to **pjsarahcollins.wordpress.com**